THE
WOODS
MURDER

A gripping crime mystery full of twists

ROY LEWIS

Revised edition 2018 by Joffe Books, London.

First published as "A Secret Singing" in 1971

www.joffebooks.com

ISBN-13: 978-1-78931-052-8

Please note this book is set in the late 1960s in England, a time before mobile phones and DNA testing, when social attitudes were very different.

Chapter 1

Most women were fascinated by Charles Lendon.

It might have been his sharp good looks, it might have been his domineering manner. It was possibly his presence: he had a way of drawing attention to himself without effort in a crowded room.

Cathy Tennant liked him, but was not *fascinated* by him.

There had been occasions when Lendon had stood close to her, almost touching her; there had been occasions when he brushed against her arm unnecessarily, held her hand overlong, looked at her in a way that principals did not or should not look at young articled clerks. There had been occasions when she had caught a glimpse of something in his eyes that she had been unable to understand — a longing, perhaps?

She had put it down to many things, to his practised gallantry, to his way with women, to her youth and his age, but she liked him, nevertheless, for he was sharp and intelligent and he looked after her professionally. He made her *work*.

It was what he did on that Friday morning. He came through into her room and smiled. 'Cathy, I've got something for you.' His voice was deep, with a practised timbre. She sometimes felt that there was something theatrical about Charles Lendon, as though he were always aware of an audience; a female audience. As he smiled, his scarred eyebrow lifted sardonically.

'Nice problem for you. Chap called Cauter. We'll be getting counsel's opinion, but it'll do you good to have a crack at it first. Let me have your notes on it and after we've taken counsel's opinion we can check one against the other. You've finished the Stephenson conveyance, haven't you?'

'Well, I'm afraid not, Mr Lendon. There's been some difficulty concerning the right of way across—'

'Hell, don't talk to me of rights of way! I've had too much trouble over the Kenton Wood affair to do other than flinch whenever I hear the words!'

He smiled again, taking the bite from the words; it was an easy, attractive smile. He'd kept his teeth in good shape.

'Anyway, when you can, Cathy. I'm out for a while now, but bring the papers in to me about three. All right?'

He touched her lightly on the shoulder before he took his leave. She turned to the papers, curiously. The details were all there. Charles Lendon's notes made it clear:

Cauter claimed to have been told by the dealer who had supplied the van that certain major repairs had been carried out to the vehicle, but within three days of taking the van, Cauter realized the repairs had not been completed.

'Mr Lendon gone out?'

Maxwell, one of the young assistant solicitors, stuck his owlish head around the door with the query.

'Yes, he won't be back until lunchtime.'

'Hmm . . . look, Cathy, I've got a couple of clients that I have to interview this morning and Parnell's equally cluttered up, so do you think you can let me have this room this morning?'

'Of course, Max. I'll go along to the library. I've got some stuff to look up anyway.'

'Ah, now then, that's another thing.' Maxwell's round eyes peered from behind his glasses at Cathy. 'It looks as though there'll be some carpenter character in there most of the morning fitting extra shelving. You're unlikely to get much peace in that room.'

'Then,' said Cathy firmly, rising to her feet with the Cauter papers, 'the only thing I can do is to use Mr Lendon's office.'

'I'm sure the old gentleman won't mind.' The sneering innuendo brought Cathy's head up, but she made no reply. Relatively old Mr Lendon might be, she thought to herself as she marched out of the room, but he still possesses yards more sex appeal than you do, young Maxwell. She went upstairs to the small room that gloried in the name of a library, where the law reports were kept, and selected a few recent volumes after browsing through the indexes under the section on Hire-Purchase. She took them, together with the Cauter papers, to Charles Lendon's room.

It was the biggest room in the office and somehow it was a reflection of the man himself. The walls were painted in a cool, dignified blue, but the Van Gogh reproduction above the fireplace presented a splash of wild, irreverent colour that typified Lendon's own character, for he was a man who, she understood, had let passion overrule prudence on more than one occasion. The furniture again was a strange contrast: the carpet was thick and wine-red, and two stiff-backed chairs stood to attention against the wall, to one side of a new leather armchair, but the second armchair, to the left of the fireplace, was deep, heavily brocaded and almost decadent in its flamboyant, sagging-seated luxury. It was Lendon's desk, however, that took her eye on this occasion.

3

Normally it was swept clean, and pristine in its appearance, its high polished surface stark but for the conventional dignity of a leather-edged blotting pad and a leather-covered pen set. This morning it was cluttered with legal papers.

Cathy stared at the desk. She could, she supposed, remove the papers and work on the desk, but she could imagine Lendon's cold anger if he returned to a disturbed surface behind which was seated an insignificant articled clerk. She had not yet felt the keen sabre-edge of Charles Lendon's anger, but she had witnessed its effects in the outer office.

The answer lay in the anteroom. She opened the door: it was a small, stuffy room that lacked ventilation but the skylight provided enough light, and she could use one of the volumes to prop open the door. The open door would give her enough air and she could work on the old roll top desk in the corner, beside the filing cabinet.

Cauter . . . Cathy settled down to the problem. She was soon immersed in it, and she was hardly aware of the passage of time. Lendon's notes of the case were admirable: it would seem that Cauter had complained to the dealer, who refused to remedy the defects or to supply another van. Cauter had then taken his complaint to the Hire-Purchase company who had loftily said that it was all a matter for Cauter and the dealer to sort out. So he stopped making payments. There was a copy of the letter written by the company solicitor, and the writ was there also. They were claiming damages for breach of the agreement. Interesting . . . Cathy stuck her pencil between her teeth and ploughed into her books.

It must have been about eleven forty-five when she realized that she needed the volume that was propping open the anteroom door. Without thinking, she crossed the room to pick it up and failed to replace it with another. The door quietly swung shut; Cathy hesitated, then decided not to bother to prop it open again since she would be finished in fifteen to twenty minutes.

She scribbled away, giving her opinion about the Cauter case. It was an interesting exercise; it would be useful to read counsel's opinion later, and indeed, to discuss it with Charles Lendon, for that matter. It was when she had just two further points to make on the sheet that she heard someone enter Charles Lendon's office.

Cathy looked up and saw the figure through the frosted glass panel of the door. It was Lendon whom she saw, and he was hanging his coat up on the pegged coat-stand in the corner. His dark figure, hazy through the glass, vanished as he went across to his desk. Cathy scribbled on, quickly; she could leave this on his desk on her way to lunch. She hoped he wouldn't be too surprised when she appeared out of the anteroom.

It was several minutes before she realized that Charles Lendon was not alone.

He used a dictating machine on occasion and at first she had assumed from his level monotone that he was speaking into it. The words were muffled through the door, and she was unable to make out what he was saying. But then she heard a lighter voice, a man's voice, answering Lendon. Again, she could make out the words only very indistinctly, but there was something familiar about the voice: it was someone she knew. What she clearly recognized, however, was the anger in the tones.

Lendon's voice remained level, but he was like that.

Anger was a passion he controlled, but it could be coldly vicious-indeed, it was probably more effective for its control. The other voice rose, however, and became almost completely inarticulate at one point. Cathy sat there in the anteroom rigidly. The quarrel in Lendon's office was not communicated to her in any detail, but it was obvious that it was serious in quality, and it was now impossible for her to leave the anteroom and walk through the office.

Occasional words drifted through to her as the man arguing with Lendon became more excited.

'. . . can't do this to me . . . lost every damned thing I've got . . . I've a good mind . . . make it all public and the hell with it!'

Cathy's face was hot, and she knew that, foolishly, she was blushing. She felt herself to be in an impossible situation: she was not eavesdropping, but she could hear the raised voices and was aware of the anger: she was not deliberately listening but she could not steal away unobserved. She could only sit there, silently, and wait. It was too late to leave now.

The voices became angrier and snatches of conversation drifted in to her.

'. . . father's money sunk into the business . . . I wish I'd never let you talk me into it in the first place!' Lendon's own measured tone had become a little deeper and more bitterly precise.

'. . . had no option to act otherwise than I did. But for me you would have been put away for a stretch of years!'

The resentment in the other's tone had reached a petulant stage, but with the petulance came a slow subsiding also, and even through the closed door Cathy became aware of the fact that whatever the argument was about Charles Lendon had the whip hand. She sat still.

She did not like her situation. The quarrel in the next room was no longer white in its heat: Lendon's tones were smooth and firm while the other man was silent. But Cathy could not escape; she could only sit and wait.

It was almost twelve-thirty when the visitor in Charles Lendon's room left. It was twelve-forty before Lendon himself went to lunch. Cathy sat on. She had a horror of emerging from the anteroom to be met by Lendon returning, having forgotten something. She couldn't bear to think of the expression that would sweep across his face in such a situation. At twelve-fifty she gathered her papers together, picked up her reference books, carefully opened the door and came out into Lendon's office. Outwardly it bore no sign of the quarrel, and yet Cathy felt that the atmosphere remained charged with an indescribable passion. It was fanciful, she knew, and the result of an over-wrought imagination, but it was an aura of unpleasantness that she was glad to escape from when she closed the door of Charles Lendon's office behind her.

She skipped down the short flight of stairs to the rooms below. She paused outside Parnell's room: had he heard the quarrel? Indeed, had any of the other office staff heard the quarrel? Probably not: the stairs tended to insulate Lendon's room from the others, and words, even white-hot words, would not travel down to other ears.

She had probably been the only person in the office to be aware of the quarrel. And even she didn't know who the other participant had been. And yet, the voice had been familiar, though roughened by anger . . .

She grimaced at herself in the mirror before she left for lunch. The straight nose wrinkled back at her, the blue eyes narrowed, the curling, unexceptional brown hair glinted in the reflected light.

'If I wanted to quarrel,' she said to her image, 'I wouldn't choose Charles Lendon to cross swords with!' But before the afternoon was out she discovered that there was more than one man in Canthorpe who wanted to cross swords with Charles Lendon.

Her principal was late returning that Friday afternoon.

When she saw him walk past her room she called out to him that she had a rough note on the Cauter case drafted.

'All right, Cathy, I'll have a look at it, but not just yet. If you'll hang on there in your room, I'll come down later and have a word with you about it. Let me have it now anyway, and I'll see you later.'

She handed the papers to him and he went upstairs.

It was three-thirty. At five-fifteen she had finished the work outstanding on the Stephenson conveyances and

Charles Lendon had still not put in an appearance. Maxwell came into the room and said cheerily: 'Well, I'm off. Not a clock-watcher of course, but it is Friday after all! Aren't you gone yet?'

The other assistant solicitor, Parnell, as tall as Maxwell was rotund, hovered in the background.

'Mr Lendon wants to have a word with me before I leave', Cathy said innocently.

'Aha!' The significance in Maxwell's exclamation caused Parnell to snigger. 'The old goat has got you staying after hours now, has he? You want us to hang on and preserve your chastity?'

Cathy stared at him without expression. The unkind thought that preservation was about all that Maxwell would be capable of came to her but was not expressed. Instead, she said: 'Someone's calling for me at five-thirty anyway.'

'Ah yes, Mike Enson, is it? Saw you together last Saturday. Well, he's big and strong enough to—'

'Oh, come on, Max, if we're going to have that beer before we head off!'

Parnell pulled Maxwell away, and Cathy rose to get her coat. There was no harm in looking ready to go — perhaps Lendon wouldn't keep her too long then.

He came downstairs only some thirty seconds later. His wicked eye glinted at her as he entered and he gave her his practised smile. 'I've got the papers, Cathy. Interesting case, isn't it? Now let's see . . .'

They stood side by side at her desk. Lendon's shoulder touched hers but she did not move away; it would be an admission that she was aware of him and this she was not prepared to do. Somehow, Charles Lendon inspired no fear in her, nor did he affect her sexually.

'Cauter . . . now you say that you think . . . ah, yes . . . that the failure of the company to go into the question of the defects with the dealer, or indeed, to sue the dealer if need be, really amounts to a failure on their part to take proper steps to mitigate the loss occasioned by Cauter's refusal to pay further instalments . . .'

He looked at her carefully, in consideration.

'Interesting point, that . . . It would mean that the company couldn't claim damages. I think we'd have to be careful in saying that, Cathy. Nevertheless . . .'

'There is a decision along these lines, you know, Mr Lendon. There's a 1960 case where—'

'You've been doing your homework,' Lendon interrupted.

There was something in his voice which made her look at him, and there was something in his eyes also which disturbed her. She could understand neither the tone nor the look; she was not familiar with Charles Lendon's armoury although she knew enough to recognize danger signals in most men, and she felt confused. She hesitated, and returned his glance in puzzlement — there was an odd, admiring expression on his face, and again, while she had seen admiration in other men's eyes when they had looked at her, this expression on Charles Lendon's face was new to her.

She opened her mouth to speak, to cover her confusion, but unexpectedly other words cut across hers.

'Can I have a word with you, Mr Lendon?'

The man who stood in the doorway was dressed in a worn grey shirt, and a brown corduroy jacket, patched at elbows and cuffs with leather. His trousers were baggy at the knees, his shoes scuffed and unpolished. He looked like a workman, returning home across town. And she knew him.

She had seen the heavy, stubble-shadowed face before, pictured in the newspaper and once on television, on the local news. A broad, sensible, quiet face that had been lined by anxiety-then. The anxiety had, within twenty-four hours, turned to anguish when the body of his nine-year-old girl had been found in Kenton Wood.

'What do you want, Mr Carson?' Charles Lendon asked in a level tone. He held himself very erect as he spoke, but with an air of careful truculence. 'I hope it's not going to be a repetition of your earlier request.'

'More or less, Mr Lendon,' Carson replied stubbornly. 'But I'm not speaking for myself, not now. I'm speaking for others. They've not sent me, or asked me to come, but—'

'But you've taken it upon yourself to come.'

'That's right,' Carson was unaffected by the sarcasm in Lendon's voice. He stood there in the doorway, a powerful, slightly hunched figure, with his arms dangling by his sides, his fingers loosely curling. He gave an impression of immobility, but Lendon was equally imperturbable. He turned away, presenting his back to Carson.

'Well, I see no point in conversation, since you already know my views.'

'I do.'

Cathy looked swiftly from one man to the other. Lendon had stiffened, and was turning his head slowly to face the man in the doorway.

'You're on my premises, Carson, and we have nothing to say to each other. I suggest you leave now, before there's trouble.'

'Trouble? Are you going to cause trouble, Lendon? To me? When you've already done all you can to ruin my life?'

Lendon's jaw was hard.

'Don't be a damned fool, Carson ! Your . . . your daughter, that was nothing to do with me—'

'That's what you've said, time and again. But it's not how the score lies in my book! And it's why I'm here now. I don't want to see it happening again to some other poor kid. You—'

Lendon's anger was rising, but characteristically he kept his voice on a level tone. 'It is my sincere hope, as it must be yours, Carson, that there will be no further incidents, but there is nothing I can do.'

'*Incidents!*'

Carson took a step forward into the room, and there was menace in the set of his shoulders. His voice was quivering with the violence of his anger. He was rapidly losing control of himself in a situation that he must have anticipated. But perhaps it was why he had come.

'Incident, you call it! Nothing you can do, you say! You know damned well that if you hadn't closed the right of way through Kenton Wood—'

'There is *no* right of way through Kenton Wood,' Lendon said icily.

'—my daughter would be alive today. And while the right of way remains closed kids will still go through the north path in the woods when they're late, or in a hurry, and one of these days the same thing's going to happen again! Some child is going to end up—'

Lendon's eyes glittered angrily; his scarred eyebrow gave him a satanic appearance. He cut Carson short with a quick gesture.

'There's no right of way across my property! Children going to the school across the main road can follow the roads. There is a bus service. There's no need for them to cross my property, and there is even less need for them to go through the north side of the woods. If only parents would accept their responsibilities and ensure that—'

Carson's anger broke. Cathy realized that in spite of his apparent calm when he had appeared in the doorway, the man must have been trembling on the edge of violence all the while; now his obvious hatred for Lendon thrust him over. He blundered forward, reaching out clumsily with a large hand, grabbing for Lendon's shoulder, but the solicitor was twisting away.

'For God's sake—' Cathy heard herself cry and then Lendon was pushing Carson past him, and stepping aside. Carson's impetus carried him sprawling across Cathy's

11

desk, a big, awkward man; Lendon remained upright, in control, lithely elegant and sneering openly. Cathy came as near to disliking Charles Lendon then as she had ever done. Lendon's voice was cutting.

'I suggest that you make yourself scarce, Carson. You're making a fool of yourself. I could already sue you for assault and battery — don't make things worse; stop this hysterical nonsense. Get out of my office!'

Carson slowly drew himself upright, one hand on the desk. He glanced towards Cathy. He seemed to have control of his anger again, and his heavy face was apologetic.

'I'm sorry, miss,' he mumbled, but she was even sorrier and felt like crying, for the look on his face was so much like the expression he had displayed in the newspaper photographs: a puzzled anxiety, a lack of comprehension as to where he had gone wrong. But even as he turned his head towards Lendon his expression was changing to one of malignity. There was no doubt as to his feelings towards Charles Lendon.

'This isn't the last you'll see or hear of me, Lendon!'

'I've no doubt!'

Carson glared at the solicitor for a long moment, and then butted his way past and out into the corridor. Lendon stood staring at the empty doorway in silence and the angry flush remained on his cheek. At last he flickered a disturbed glance towards Cathy: he was obviously unhappy that she should have witnessed the brawl with Carson.

'We'll leave this now,' he said, gesturing towards the Cauter papers. 'We can take the matter up again on Monday.'

Cathy nodded and put on her coat. Lendon assisted her, his fingers lingering unnecessarily on her shoulder. He made no further reference to Carson. His breathing had slowed again and he was in full control of himself. He stood aside, and Cathy preceded him to the door.

'Can I give you a lift home?' he asked suddenly, and to her surprise, a little hesitantly. Hesitancy in Charles Lendon seemed out of character.

'No, thank you, Mr Lendon. Someone's waiting for me. I hope he is, at least!' She said it with a brief smile, as she turned away. Just inside the main doors, Lendon put a hand on her arm.

'Someone waiting? Who is it?' Cathy was taken aback at the urgency in his tone, for she saw no reason for it. On the other hand she saw no reason why he should not know. 'A young man called Enson; Mike Enson. And in fact, there he is now! Good night, Mr Lendon.'

She walked quickly across to the sports car drawn up at the kerb on the other side of the road. She got in with a brief apology to Mike for keeping him waiting, but he hardly seemed to hear her. He was looking away from her, glaring back coldly towards the offices of Lendon, Philips and Barrett.

And when Cathy followed his gaze she saw that Charles Lendon was still standing on the steps of the office. He in his turn was staring at the car, and at Mike Enson. Even at this distance Cathy could see the expression of enmity that shadowed Charles Lendon's features.

Chapter 2

It was a pleasant room full of dark wood and whorled glass and dim lights, and it was a room made for lovers. But just loving wasn't enough. These surroundings held memories for Cathy, for Mike had brought her here several times. They had come out of the cold wind and they had sat in front of the fire nursing their drinks and the silences had held them in a warm contentment.

Those silences had been loving silences, times to savour what they had come to mean to each other, to think about how it had been and how it would be without each other, to think how it was going to be, together.

But tonight it was different and just loving wasn't enough.

The silences that drifted between them were cold anger in an icy sea of disapproval. Cathy had come to believe that such problems could be overcome; the silences and the awkwardness of explanations and the difficulties of a new relationship could usually be smoothed over by the fact of loving, but not always, and that Friday evening after she had witnessed Lendon's quarrel with Carson was one of those evenings when a smoothing over was impossible.

Cathy glared in silence towards the flaring hearth while Mike stared moodily at the brass horse buckles winking fulsomely above the stone fireplace. She snorted and sipped at her lager.

She had met Mike Enson a month ago when the heavy frosts of late January had turned to a cold February rain. He'd come along a few minutes after a careless driver had drenched her with a great bow wave of puddle water lying above an overflowing drain and she'd been soaked from head to foot. As she came out of the side road Mike Enson, in his sports car, had come squealing to a violent halt, spattering her with thick mud as he did so.

Cathy had stood there speechless, shoulders hunched and arms stiffly held out in front of her, glowering at him as he thrust his fair head out of the passenger window.

He looked her up and down with a studied casualness that she found infuriating. It was not only his surprised air; it was the fact that water was running down her neck and squelching into her shoes. She clenched her fists impotently, and waited.

'By God,' he had said, 'I've seen nothing more like a drowned rat in my life!'

'You just splashed me!'

'You mean it made any *difference*?' he had enquired, raising his eyebrows. And she had noticed his friendly, slate-grey eyes even through the soaking despondency of her frustration and anger. Then he grinned and she liked his wide mouth, and smile, too.

'You'd better get in, and let me drive you home. In your state you're quite likely to float there, but this way it'll be quicker.'

She had hesitated for only a moment; it would have been morally satisfying to snub him but physically foolish to so indulge her ego. She was damned wet. She got in the car.

'I never did like sports cars.' The words were by way of salve to her outrage.

'You obviously prefer walking in the rain. You must have been out in it for a week!' When she extracted the small mirror from her handbag she could see what he meant. Her dark hair was plastered to her muddy face under the sodden headscarf and there were dirty stains all over her raincoat.

'By God, you don't half smell too,' he commented cheerfully. 'My name's Mike Enson, by the way.'

Fury overrode politeness and she glowered silently at her mirror. Warm air filtered a little comfort around her squelching feet, but she refused its solace, and Enson drove on silently until they reached the outskirts of the town.

'Well,' he suggested, cheerful still, 'if not names, at least an address, otherwise, where do I drop you? The nearest pond?'

'I was half drowned by a lunatic road hog who almost killed me. I do not get wet as a hobby. My name is Cathy Tennant, and I live in a flat in Camden Street.'

'And I'm delighted to meet you.'

He illustrated his delight by calling on her two evenings later and she made little attempt to conceal her own pleasure.

It had been a marvellous month in many ways, lifted by the exhilaration of their realizing just what they had come to mean to each other, but it had culminated in something quite unexpected. Mike had asked her to marry him, and she had turned him down.

Cathy plonked the glass of lager down on the table to her right and glared defiantly at Mike, sitting beside her. 'I didn't really turn you down you know, not flatly.'

'As good as,' he disagreed. 'No matter. Let's just forget it.'

'I don't want to forget it! Why are you being so damned pig-headed?'

'Pig-headed? I'm being pig-headed? What the hell is there to describe *your* conduct?'

'Lower your voice. We're being stared at!'

'You call me pig-headed, but as soon as I try to come back at you, you tell me to shut up—'

'I didn't say shut up, I said—'

'-when all the time it's you who—'

'-was that you were speaking too loudly and—'

'-is being pig-headed in refusing to give me what I regard as an adequate reason for turning me down.'

Cathy pursed her lips; Mike folded his arms across his chest and glowered. 'You said you were in love with me.'

'That's got nothing to do with it.'

'It's got *everything* to do with it!'

'Mike, please!'

Suddenly, she was near to tears, and he saw it, and he put his hand out to her but this only made things worse so she grabbed for his handkerchief and blew into it violently. When she looked up there was the hint of a smile at the corner of his mouth, and his eyes had softened.

'Sometimes I think you're just like a kid,' he said quietly.

'Just because I'm only twenty and you're eight years older!'

But the earlier rancour had left their voices, and they looked at each other and she thought that perhaps it would be all right after all. It was a drawback in their relationship, a difficulty that they would have to surmount, this strange barrier that occasionally rose between them. A failure to communicate, a failure to reach each other verbally, that was it; it was a failure that they could bypass as they were bypassing it now, by the very fact that they were in love and people in love had their own imaginations and their own conceptual methods of communication: a look, a touch, a breath. This was how it was now, a glance and things were getting better, even though explanations would yet be necessary. The atmosphere was easier, and communication might again be possible, where it had proved impossible only moments before.

'We've not known each other long, Cathy.'

'A month.'

'It's happened quickly, this love thing.'

'It's happened just right.'

'But you won't marry me.'

'I won't marry you . . . *yet*. You didn't let me get out that last word last time. It's a very important word.'

'The difference between a positive and a negative. But it doesn't explain anything.'

Cathy reached out and took his hand. It was a strong hand that in a way was typical of Mike. He exuded strength, even though he was not heavily built, strength and reliability. Though there had been occasions when he had seemed almost weak and very vulnerable. But those were private occasions the thought of which now caused her knees to tremble.

'You've got to understand, Mike, I love you and I hope we will marry. But not yet. It's too early.'

'Cathy, I'm twenty-eight, I'm a qualified surveyor, I'm earning £2,000 a year, I should soon get a partnership. . .hell, I can support a family, why can't we get married?'

'Because you're qualified — and I'm not.'

Mike groaned.

'What the hell does that matter? Look, Cathy, I want a wife, not a breadwinner. It doesn't matter a damn whether you get qualified or not. I want you to bring up my kids, not trouble the Inland Revenue authorities!'

'You're being old-fashioned, and you haven't got the point,' Cathy insisted stubbornly. 'I *want* to qualify-and I'm going to qualify.'

'All right, why don't we get married and—'

'And *after* I qualify, I'll marry.'

Mike's mouth took a grimmer line. 'If I'm still around.'

'If you loved me, you'd still be around.'

Mike grunted despondently.

'I suppose you're right at that.'

She squeezed his hand.

'Please try to see my point of view over this matter. Dad keenly wanted me to get a professional qualification if I wasn't going to university. And he's right-because if we married, and you died . . . well come on, Mike, it *could* happen — and I was left alone, or with children to bring up, what could I do? If I had nothing behind me but seven years at school? He's right when he says that getting a professional qualification is important, and that's why he got me the interviews, that's why he arranged for the interview here at the firm, and that's why he'd be against my marrying before I qualified.'

'You mean it's your father who—'

'It's *my* idea, Mike. My idea and my responsibility. In just eighteen months I'll have finished my period of articles. Provided I get through the Part II exams this coming summer I'll become an admitted solicitor. Thereafter, any time you ask me to marry you I'll do so gladly. But until then, I must refuse. If I marry now, who knows what would happen? Maybe I'd never get to my exams, maybe I'd lose the incentive to work, I don't know. But I do know what I'm capable of now, and I've got to stick the course.'

Mike looked at her calmly, with a twisted half smile on his face.

'You're a stubborn girl, Cathy Tennant. You know your own mind. I can't argue with you.'

'I'm glad. On this matter at least, argument will do no good. My mind is made up. It's right for me, and for Dad, and, well, for us, too, in the long run. Apart from that, there's Mr Lendon—'

'Lendon?' A certain harshness crept into his voice. 'Where does Lendon come into this?' Cathy looked at him in surprise, raising her eyebrows at his tone.

'Well, you know perfectly well that I'm articled to Lendon. He's bound to come into it!' Mike drained his glass of beer before replying. His eyes were slate-cold, and they held a vicious gleam.

'I see no reason why you need to consider his interests at all.'

'Mike! I don't think that's fair! Of course I have to consider his interests! He's my principal, he's helped me a great deal — for believe me, there are many principals who give their clerks no help whatsoever—'

'You mean he's had you ensconced alone with him in his little office when the rest of the staff are gone, don't you?'

'Don't be so ridiculous,' Cathy said, half amused, half exasperated. 'I tell you he's been very kind, and very helpful, more than I could expect—'

'I've no doubt!'

She paused, and a little of the old anger seeped back as she caught the inflection in Mike's voice and saw the bitter sneer on his face.

'And moreover, I have a duty to him under the terms of my employment. I have an agreement with him to work out my articles. He's kept his side of the bargain; I must keep mine. I've got a place in his office — he entrusts me with a great deal of work, and a great deal of responsibility. If I were to leave the firm I would not only be leaving an excellent training ground for myself, but I'd be leaving his office in a certain amount of difficulty. He relies upon me, he's come to look upon me as—'

'As *what,* Cathy?'

There was no mistaking the implication in his tone and Cathy's surprise was matched only by her hurt. For some reason Mike was making something of her relationship with Lendon, making something unpleasant of it — and she knew that he could know nothing that would make such an inference remotely possible.

'I think you should explain yourself, Mike.'

'Why should I go on the defensive? You explain *yourself,* Cathy.' She released his hand with dignity.

'I don't know what you mean by explain. Charles Lendon is my principal. We have a working relationship. He looks upon me as an assistant solicitor rather than as an articled clerk. He treats me professionally and with respect.'

'He's never treated *any* woman with respect!'

'Charles Lendon treats me with professional courtesy and respect. Charles Lendon is about thirty years older than I am—'

'Hell's bells!' Mike groaned. 'Do you think that makes any difference at all? Don't you know Lendon's reputation? Don't you know that—'

Cathy stood up.

'There are many things I don't know; there are some things I do not care to know.'

She was conscious of heads turning at the bar behind her but she was angry. It was an anger unlike her previous mood of desperation: this anger was cold, and precise.

'I've no idea what you're seeking to imply, Mike, and I don't care. I work for Charles Lendon; he's kind to me, professionally, and I have no reason to question his conduct in other directions. I want to talk no more about it now. I'd like to go home.'

Mike rose to stand beside her. He seemed disturbed — his face was flushed. He fumbled awkwardly with his coat as they moved towards the door and only Cathy replied to the barman's good night. They walked in silence across to the car and Mike held the door open for her as she climbed in. When he took the driver's seat beside her she said nothing. The bonnet of the car sparkled whitely under the moon. Mike pulled on his gloves and shivered, then looked at her.

'It's almost as frosty outside,' he said gently, 'as it is in here.'

Cathy huddled into her coat and made no reply.

'I'm sorry, Cathy,' he tried again, but she could bring herself only to incline her head slightly, in recognition of his apology. It seemed to satisfy him to a little extent at least, for he nodded in his turn and then started the engine.

'I am sorry,' he said, 'believe me. It's just that I know Lendon — and I know his reputation. And if I thought that he'd laid a hand on you I'd break his damned neck!'

Chapter 3

Lendon, Philips and Barrett was not an old-established firm of solicitors. It did not have the background that many of the firms in Canthorpe possessed. The other firms had been built up on a basis of trust and litigation work, for in the nineteenth century there had been little to gain from the monopoly of conveyancing since relatively little land changed hands. When it did, of course, the work was remunerative with each page of a verbose conveyance being charged for separately. But when Lendon, Philips and Barrett was formed times had changed. It was 1942, some years after the Law Society obtained the right to make rules of professional conduct, some years after solicitors were forced to keep their clients' money in a separate account from their own, and shortly after solicitors were required by law to produce an auditor's certificate on their accounts when applying for renewal of the annual practising certificate.

Charles Lendon had qualified in 1937, but the war had called him, albeit briefly. He was invalided out in 1941, a major, with a scar above his right eye from exploding shrapnel, a piece of which remained embedded in his head near the brain. Too close to justify the risk of an operation, it caused his release from the army, but in a sense it added to his appearance: the scar gave a devil-may-care lift to his eyebrow that went well with his general appearance — lean, athletic, nervy. He was a little above middle height, and rather short in his speech with fools. He joined Philips and Barrett in their firm and the old gentlemen were only too glad to see him. They welcomed his glamour, his incisiveness and his capacity for attracting lucrative business. The assiduity with which Charles Lendon made and maintained contacts on the social and professional plane illustrated perfectly that the rule of etiquette which prevented solicitors from advertising or touting for business need in no way inhibit the flood of new work that came in.

But this did not deny the fact also that there were occasions when Charles Lendon was somewhat of an embarrassment to the firm. He could be a charming man, and was a handsome one, and a sound businessman, but he was not without his weaknesses. They became apparent during the early years: old Barrett, just before he died, had been heard to say that if Lendon could only have sublimated his sexual drive into other channels he could have become Prime Minister. As it was, it seemed in the 1940s that Charles Lendon's ambitions lay largely in the field of sexual athleticism. And old Barrett's hope that the whole thing was something that Lendon would grow out of was never fulfilled.

It was true that Lendon's conduct became tempered with discretion in later years: his earlier canters had been open and fearless of convention, but his later outings were at least more circumspect. He had learned to cool his passion with an element of caution.

Philips, the other partner, worried little about Lendon.

His reaction had always been — 'Don't give a damn whether a man wears a coloured waistcoat, a moustache or another man's wife as long as he does his job well,' and it was a precept which he clung to until he also died, in 1949, leaving Lendon as senior partner and Brian, old man Philips's son, as a recently qualified junior-some years younger than Lendon and nowhere near his peer in efficiency.

During the 1950s the firm doubled its profits and although assistant solicitors were employed none were taken into partnership: Lendon used them for a few years and when they became insistent in their claims he advised them that a move would be in their interest. Brian Philips remained quietly in the background; he knew his place, he was the sort of man who would always know his place. It cried out from his pale blue eyes, so unlike Lendon's piercing grey, and it was apparent from his over-precise dressing, his fussy attention to personal detail, his inability to hold another man's eyes for any length of time, his continued assumption that he was in danger of offending the client with whom he dealt. He knew his place . . . and yet there were times when he spoke to Lendon, times when the flicker in his eyes held an emotion positive enough to amount even to dislike when he looked at his senior partner. Entirely negative people rarely held positive emotions so to that extent Brian Philips could not be regarded as negative.

The 1950s had gone and the booming years of the sixties were slipping past. The firm was prospering. Two assistant solicitors were taken on and Cathy Tennant joined the firm as an articled clerk. A month later Brian Philips surprisingly left Lendon, Philips and Barrett and set up in practice on his own account on the other side of town. Lendon was now sole principal. Properties changed hands, wills were drawn up, contracts were sealed, marriages begun and ended. The Canthorpe Borough Police Force was amalgamated with the County Constabulary and January came in bitter and cold. One frosty morning Jenny Carson was brutally murdered in Kenton Wood; a week later Mike Enson fell in love with

25

Cathy Tennant. But Charles Lendon remained the same; the years had changed him but little. He had kept his attitudes, his flair, his figure, his looks, his respected position in the community . . . and his appetite for women. He had never married.

Perhaps this was why there seemed to be no one to mourn for him when he was found at the Old Mill above Insterley, five days after the quarrel with Carson, with his sightless eyes wide and glazed and a twelve-inch rusty steel skewer in his heart.

Chapter 4

Three locally born villagers out at Hamberley had told Chief Constable Rogers that he would pay for his rashness in. pruning his roses so early. It was all very well, they said, it was all very well pruning at the first sight of a warm spring sun, but the frosts weren't over yet and at Hamberley the frosts could tear the heart out of a rose-bush. So Chief Constable Rogers gnawed at his lip and worried and realized that he hadn't shaved too well that morning, as he touched the stubble just below the curve of his chubby chin. He shook his head.

'It would be a mistake,' he murmured.

Detective Chief Superintendent Simpson scowled. The expression on his face had put the fear of death into more than a few villains over the years, married as it was to a massive, broad-shouldered frame and huge, cruel hands. Yet to date its effect upon Chief Constable Rogers had been one of irritation only: Rogers was of the new school that believed in using a psychological key to open a door rather than a bludgeon to batter it down.

Simpson prowled around the room like a restless cat. He carried his head low, belligerently.

'I think we can handle it . . . no, I'm damn *sure* we can handle it!' he said with a trace of anger in his tone.

'And I'm equally convinced that we have more than enough on our plate already. Now be reasonable, Hugh!'

Rogers knew even as he said it that reasonableness had nothing at all to do with the matter: it was almost eight months now since Hugh Simpson had reached his present rank and he had yet to lose the novelty of the flavour of power that it gave him. Simpson was aware of his rank on all conceivable occasions: Rogers guessed he even took it to bed with him, and the thought caused a smile to touch his lips at the possibilities presented by such a situation.

Unfortunately, Simpson saw the smile and though he could in no way guess its import he was obviously angered.

'You think the force isn't up to it!' he said and marched across to the window. 'Well, I think it is, and I think that if you don't agree to handing this over to us it'll be a serious blow to morale!'

The chief constable rose and came from behind his desk to walk across to the window and stand beside the irate chief superintendent. He looked up at Simpson: the man was a good three inches taller than he, and said in the most soothing tones he could muster: 'Hugh, you must know that I have every confidence in the force. You fully realize that I am aware of the quality of the manpower we have. But you've got to see reason on this thing. Let us just look at the facts. It's not more than a year now since we amalgamated the county force with the Canthorpe Borough force. This in itself has caused problems — on the other hand, it accounts in part for your promotion, as you well know. But we still haven't achieved the rationalization nor the slickness that a really fine force can muster, and until then we must tread with care. This is not a game — people are involved.'

'I would be the last,' Simpson said stiffly, 'to suggest that it was a *game*, sir.'

The word had been badly chosen, Rogers admitted to himself. Neither the Force nor life itself was a game to Simpson: he was a hard, dedicated and ruthless man. Rogers sighed.

'All right, I agree that I need hardly remind you of our public duties. You will accept on the other hand that the amalgamation poses certain problems. Allied to that is the Carson case.'

'But—'

'Please, Hugh, let me finish. When the Carson girl was murdered we were presented with a bombshell. You know very well what a case of this nature can mean: the publicity alone when a nine-year-old girl is assaulted and brutally murdered is enormous. The pressures brought upon us as a result are tremendous — every man in the force feels *involved*. And when there is no result after eight weeks of investigation—'

'Sir—'

'When, as I say, there is no result, the pressure remains and becomes more difficult to handle, if only because it becomes less strident but more personal, more nerve-sapping in its effects. So—'

'So you don't think we can handle the Lendon killing.'

'I haven't said that, Hugh. I haven't said or intimated that the force can't handle the Lendon killing. All I'm saying is that with the Carson enquiry still in our laps . . . and you'll remember I gave you your head over that . . . it would be extremely unwise to ask you and the others to take upon yourselves the added burden of this Lendon matter. It's too much. I think that there is only one course open to us.'

'I believe, sir, that you're underestimating the force. And I repeat, if we're not called upon to handle the Lendon killing it'll be a severe blow to morale. All I ask is—'

'The answer is no, Hugh. And I don't underestimate the difficulties. As far as I can see, it's you who are over-estimating the capabilities of our young force.'

Simpson turned to glare at the chief constable. His mouth was hard with disappointment; it was obvious that he was taking Rogers's refusal as a personal matter, a vote of no confidence.

'Look, sir, I'm *sure* we can handle it. I know the Carson thing's dragging on, but it'll be only a matter of days before something breaks there. We do have three leads, as you know. And the Lendon killing, if you'll only give me twenty-four hours at it I'm sure—'

'No.'

Chief Constable Rogers injected the relevant amount of firmness into his tone to illustrate that as far as he was concerned the matter was decided. He turned away from the window and took up a more official position behind his desk.

'I've given my reasons, Hugh. I think it would be unwise to burden the force with two investigations at once.'

'But twenty-four hours only!'

Rogers looked at the chief superintendent coldly.

'You plead a lost cause, Superintendent, and you show a surprising lack of regard for the ratepayers. You know as well as I that in a murder investigation the situation is quite clear. We handle it ourselves, or we call in the murder squad from Scotland Yard. If we handle it, we pay the costs. If we call in Scotland Yard the cost is shared. But shared only if we call them in within twenty-four hours: otherwise, calling them in at a later date means that the costs are dumped straight into our laps. I see little value in asking our ratepayers to bear the full costs of the Lendon enquiry simply to satisfy your ego.'

Simpson's back stiffened. 'Sir?'

'That is how I see it.' The chief constable's tone was calm. 'You already have your hands full with the Carson enquiry. You think that you should be allowed to handle the Lendon case too, and you regard it as an affront to you personally that I've decided to call in Scotland Yard, an affront to you and the force. I regard such feelings on your part as egotistical. Not that it makes any difference. I've reached my decision. We'll be asking for the assistance of the murder squad.'

'Yes, sir.'

Simpson's craggy, lined face was impassive as he stood to attention. Rogers recognized the implied rebuke in the man's stance and lack of expression. He sighed relenting.

'Don't take it so damned hard, Hugh. You're new to your rank, you've plenty on your plate, and this Carson thing should be more than enough to drive any man into his grave with overwork. You're far too valuable a man to be asked to dissipate his efforts over two investigations when you can concentrate upon, and get results in, one.'

It was obvious that Simpson remained unconvinced.

Rogers glowered at the chief superintendent. Every man had his faults, and with Simpson it was overconfidence, a prickly sense of injustice, an easily wounded pride and an overconsciousness of his rank. They were rough edges that the years might smooth away, but Rogers doubted it.

'Just one more thing I have to say. I shall expect you to render every assistance to the man who is sent from Scotland Yard.'

'Of course, sir.'

Of course. It went without saying, really. After all, hadn't they both agreed that this wasn't a game, a power play, a jockeying for position? The chief constable turned back to his desk and nodded as Simpson made his way out. A good officer, Simpson: brash, violent, and over-weening, but a good policeman.

In the corridor outside the chief constable's room Chief Superintendent Simpson lit a cigarette. His hand shook slightly with the anger that he still found some difficulty in controlling. He strode down the corridor and pushed through the door at the far end. A startled detective-constable hastily tried to push aside the newspaper he had been reading surreptitiously, but Simpson ignored him and thrust through the room and into his own office. He slammed the door behind him and with a quick petulance kicked the waste-paper basket aside before slumping down into the chair behind his desk. He glared moodily at the papers on his desk, and ground out the cigarette in the ashtray. It had hardly been smoked.

There was a light tap on the door, and Detective-Sergeant Turner entered with a murmured apology to place some more papers on the chief superintendent's desk. He turned to go but when he reached the door he hesitated, then looked back to the chief superintendent, hunched and glowering behind his desk.

'Er . . . what's happening, sir?'

Simpson didn't look up. His fist was balled on the desk and he was staring at it. Turner waited, but when Chief Superintendent Simpson's reply came, it was with a snarl. 'What's happening? The chief constable — he's calling in the bloody Mets!'

Chapter 5

The murder of Charles Lendon had had an electric effect upon the office of Lendon, Philips and Barrett that Thursday morning. The receptionist, Stella, was bubbling in the way only a seventeen-year-old girl can bubble with excitement. The three legal executives had held a short meeting of their own, decided to go about their business as efficiently as usual and keep the junior clerical staff in their places and hard at work. The two assistant solicitors, Parnell and Maxwell, had undertaken a long discussion as to what they should now do since the firm was without a principal, looked very serious and hinted at Charles Lendon's sexual proclivities in hushed tones, and suggested to Cathy that it might well have had something to do with his murder. And hadn't he *ever* made a pass at her?

Cathy was conscious of the subtle implication behind their remarks. She was perfectly aware that if she as much as flickered an eyelid in the direction of either young bachelor he would have taken his chance with both hands.

Literally, she thought.

Cathy was surprised to see Brian Philips at the office that first morning after the solicitor's body was discovered. Philips had not returned to the firm since he had relinquished his share in the partnership; Cathy suspected that he had quarrelled with Lendon. Now he stuck his head around Cathy's door and said in his characteristic quiet tones:

'Hallo, Cathy. You'll have heard the news, of course.'

'Who hasn't?'

The office itself had buzzed all morning and no work had been done. All the office staff had expected a sudden deluge of policemen armed with notebooks, but it was now almost mid-day and none had arrived. The effervescent excitement had remained, if a little flat at the edges and less frothy, but it was with a certain sense of anticlimax that Cathy spoke to Philips.

He came in and sat down. His mousy hair dipped over his forehead in a manner quite foreign to him: he was usually so careful about his personal appearance, but the events of the morning had obviously had their effect upon him.

'I've just got back from the police station,' he said, flickering a nervous smile in Cathy's direction. 'As soon as I heard this morning that Charles had been found murdered up at Insterley, I thought I'd better go straight around to the station to see what information I could offer.'

'Do they have any idea-?'

'None at all, as far as I know.' Philips shook his head in a curious, birdlike manner. 'And it would seem they're not going to handle it themselves. They're going to call in a man from Scotland Yard. I suppose in a way it's better; you know, a fresh, objective look at a community can lead to things being seen that an insider wouldn't perceive. I mean, you, Cathy, you probably have a clearer idea as to what goes on around here in Canthorpe than have many residents with forty or fifty years chalked up. You've lived here, what? . . . Two, three years? Ever since you came here as an articled clerk, isn't it? You've brought with you the sort of outsider's vision that people like me lack.'

He looked miserably down at his hands.

'Poor Charles . . . A meat skewer. You know, he would have hated the crudity of that.' The suspicion of a smile hovered over his lips and it brought her up with a jolt. Brian.

Philips remained in the room with her for almost another fifteen minutes but she was hardly aware of him, hardly aware of what he talked about. The thought and the memory of that secret smile remained with her while he talked.

'Of course, all this puts you people in a difficult position. I mean, Charles was the sole partner, and now you'll be without a principal. Parnell and Maxwell will carry on for a while I suppose, but they can't be regarded as your employers. Maybe they'll set up on their own account, perhaps take this place over, buy it from Charles's executors. I wonder who he left it to . . . he made a will, I suppose. However . . .' His eyes flickered away from Cathy and he looked around the room. 'I've not been back here for some time now . . .'

He jumped suddenly as the door opened. Parnell looked in. 'Police've arrived. They'll be wanting a chat with each of us later.'

'I'll be on my way now then,' Philips murmured. He left quietly, but she remembered his remark about Charles Lendon long after he'd gone and, in some unaccountable way, it saddened her.

It was no use trying to explain it to Mike when they sat in the car on Tarlock Hill that evening.

'I don't see why *you* have to cry over Charles Lendon! You'll be almost alone if you do.'

'That's not a pleasant thing to say. Charles Lendon was an efficient man and—'

'And always *right*. They're the most uncomfortable kind to deal with. But you sound as though you're a member of the Lendon Fan Club.'

Cathy struggled free of his encircling arm. 'I don't understand you. Why are you so bitter about him?'

'I'm not. He's dead. Some will say good riddance.'

'But he was *murdered*, Mike. How can you say that?'

'The fact that he was murdered simply illustrates that someone hated his guts, hated him enough to remove him.'

The venom in his tone disturbed her; to cover her confusion she asked him for a cigarette. They sat side by side and the glow of their cigarettes dimly lit the interior of the car.

'Did the police come to the office this morning?'

'A detective-constable came in and looked around Lendon's room, locked it and took the key.'

'No questions?'

'No questions. I gather a detective will be in tomorrow to do that. A man from Scotland Yard. They're waiting for him.'

Mike laughed. There was an uncharacteristic harshness about the sound. 'I wonder when he'll get around to questioning me.'

'You? What would they do that for?'

Mike laughed again but it was still not a natural laugh. 'Nothing, really. But . . . well, I did know Lendon and I made no secret of my dislike for him, so I suppose they'll get around to grilling me eventually.'

'*Grilling* you?'

He was suddenly impatient. 'Aw, the hell with it, Cathy! I'm not saying I've anything to tell them, I'm just saying they might want to question me! It was an innocent remark — don't harp on it! They'll want to see you too won't they?'

'Yes, but—'

'No buts. In a murder investigation policemen behave like ferrets. They start poking their narrow little noses down all sorts of burrows, they sniff out all sorts of secrets, they ask all kinds of questions. And some of the questions will hurt because they'll drag out into the open old dead quarrels, and quarrels not so dead, too. Muck gets raked up. Dirt gets stirred. The whole thing can be bloody unpleasant, particularly when what's stirred up has no real relevance to the murder enquiry anyway.'

It wasn't merely impatience, Cathy suddenly realized. It was fear.

Chapter 6

The unfortunate thing about knees was that when they were bent they presented a bony appearance. This could be doubly unfortunate when the knees in question were extremely bony to begin with. But Detective Chief Inspector Crow had long ago finished worrying about his knees or indeed about his general appearance. He was perfectly well aware of the impression that he made when entering a room full of strangers. He was more than used to the turning heads, the lull in the conversation, and the occasional nervous giggle. In a way he didn't mind this, for he saw himself in the mirror each morning and he was forced to admit that his domed skull did present a most unprepossessing sight, and when it was allied to the jutting, prominent nose, the deep-set eyes, and supported by the scrawny neck and tall thin framework of his body, upon which clothes dangled rather than were worn, he could hardly expect people to behave otherwise than rudely.

Chief Constable Rogers was of the old school, however, thought Crow to himself. Rogers didn't even blink when Crow walked in; he simply extended his hand

and indulged in small talk as naturally as though he were dealing with an old friend.

'And have you got your hotel?'

'Thank you, yes,' Crow replied with a smile. 'Wilson and I are staying at the Warwick Arms. It seems more than comfortable.'

'You'll appreciate what I mean when I say that I hope your stay won't be extended.'

'Quite.'

Crow observed the chubby chief constable warily. He would not have a great deal to do with the man, for the Lendon investigation was Crow's responsibility and both he and Rogers knew that interference would be unthinkable. Nevertheless, Crow felt it was necessary to get to know Rogers reasonably well; when one of the murder squad came into a provincial area like this it could cause friction, and it would have to be the chief constable who would be keeping his men in check. Rogers was worried, that was obvious, but at the moment Crow was prepared to accept that the cause of his anxiety would simply be that he had two unsolved murders on his patch. . . and that was two too many.

'It's been kind of you to see me so soon,' Crow said, rising to his feet to tower over the chief constable, 'I'll detain you no longer, sir. I'll get on with what we have—'

'I've asked Chief Superintendent Simpson to hang on in his office for a word with you. He'll have told the scene-of-crime unit to stand by for your orders, and I expect he'll have been on to forensics as well.'

'I imagine,' Crow said quietly, 'that Detective-Sergeant Wilson will already have detailed the unit. I'll be spending the morning down at Lendon's office, myself. I can leave the scene-of-crime stuff to Wilson. But I'd like to meet the chief superintendent, sir. I imagine he's handling the other murder on your hands.'

'The Jenny Carson case, yes,' muttered Rogers. 'All right. Look, I'll take you through to Hugh Simpson's office and you can have a quick word with him there. Oh, damn!'

The telephone on his desk was jangling. The chief constable grabbed it, listened, then made a face at Crow. He covered the mouthpiece and said: 'Can you find your own way there, Inspector?'

'Of course.'

Crow withdrew, leaving Rogers to his telephone conversation. The officer at the desk pointed out the chief superintendent's room and Crow, declining his offer of an escort, knocked on the door. Hearing no reply, he knocked a second time, opened the door and looked in.

The big man behind the desk had a glass of water in his hand and his head was thrown back so that the cord-like veins stood out in his thick neck. He was red in the face. A gargling sound issued from his throat. As he saw Crow he swallowed the liquid, and swung around in his chair with a curse.

'What the hell do you want? Don't you believe in knocking?'

Crow paused, as he noted that the chief superintendent was not of the Rogers school: the man's eyes grew round with disbelief as he took in the details of Crow's hairless skull.

'I am Detective Chief Inspector Crow.'

'Good God!'

It was only with an effort that Simpson pulled himself together. Crow was not offended: he had no illusions about his appearance though he obviously preferred the reaction of Rogers to the undisciplined lack of control of Simpson. The chief superintendent rubbed a hand over his throat and scowled. The expression deepened the lines of his craggy face and drew his bushy eyebrows together.

'Come in, Crow. Siddown. I've got a sore throat. Out all yesterday evening.'

'The Carson murder?'

Simpson's face darkened, unpredictably. 'Why do you ask?'

Take off my dumping boots, Crow thought to himself. We have to tread warily; there are tender toes here. Before he had time to frame his reply, Simpson continued:

'No, it was Lendon, in fact. Someone had to sort things out up there. You weren't around to do it. Someone had to get things organized.'

'Yes.' Crow sat down, and Simpson peered at him with overt suspicion. 'Anyway,' he grumbled, 'it's your pigeon now.'

'That's right. It's my pigeon.'

Crow looked carefully at the chief superintendent, sitting there caressing his throat. He decided that he'd better sound out the waters somewhat.

'The Lendon murder, coming on top of this other enquiry, will have occasioned some publicity problems, no doubt. I imagine that you'll have had the press breathing down your neck on the—'

Simpson swung his chair to face Crow squarely. His lips were set in a thin line, and his eyes were hard as he glared at Crow.

'I think we'd better get things clear, Chief Inspector. Right from the start. I'm tied up with the Carson enquiry but I can handle it, and I could have handled the Lendon case too, with one hand tied behind my back. I didn't want the Mets called in, but they were, and you're here, and it's your pigeon. If you're worried about public pressure, I'm not. If you can't face the newspaper hounds, hard luck. But it's your problem, the whole Lendon thing. Your problem, Chief Inspector.'

'You will, of course, offer the customary assistance.' Crow's expression was bland.

'Of course. Office, two men assigned, use of lab people and scene-of-crime unit. But remember, Crow, they've got another case on their hands too. My case. And they're my boys, so it's as well that they know what their priorities must be, from the start. They've got to work for me, and it's a case then of devil take the hindmost.'

Crow sat very still.

'You make it sound like a race.'

It was possible that Simpson was misled by the quietness of Crow's reply. He didn't know Crow well enough to understand the significance of the mild tones used by the murder squad man.

'You can damn well regard it in that light or any other,' Simpson said with confidence. 'All I'm emphasizing is that if you want any of the force other than the two assigned you'd better come through me and then I'll clear it for them.'

'And what of emergencies?'

'I can't see any emergencies arising where it'll be necessary to act otherwise than through me. If you'll just make your request—'

'I'm sorry, that won't do.'

'What won't do?'

Crow ignored the belligerence in Simpson's tone. 'The arrangements that you suggest will not be acceptable. I'm afraid that I cannot possibly act through you. I require the usual services from the force in this investigation. I'm extremely grateful for the two men assigned, but I've no doubt I'll need others from time to time and particularly to begin with. I appreciate that you will need to exercise a co-ordinating function, but I cannot possibly come through you for everything I need.'

'Well, you'll bloody well have to!'

'We differ in our assessment of the situation, I fear.'

There was a short silence in the room. Simpson was staring at Crow as though he could hardly believe his ears. Slowly the chief superintendent rose and took advantage of the fact to stand over Crow.

'I think,' he said thickly, 'we need to get a few things sorted out.'

'I agree.'

'Such as the fact that you are acting under a provincial—'

'I'm sorry, you meant *with*, rather than under, didn't you?'

Simpson's face was reddening; the flush spread like a slow-moving stain across the rough skin of his face.

'The first thing I have to do, obviously, Inspector Crow, is remind you of my rank!'

'No, sir. The first thing that *you* have to do is to remind yourself that your rank is irrelevant: I am in charge of the Lendon investigation, at the request of this division. I shall require the usual courtesies, the usual assistance. I shall conduct the investigation. I shall answer in no way to you for its conduct and I shall in no way work through you. I appreciate that the force is involved in two murder cases; I shall bear this in mind in my demands upon the manpower available. But I cannot place myself in the position where I have to come cap in hand every time I want to make use of the force.'

Crow received the impression that it was a long time since a subordinate in rank had addressed Simpson in a critical fashion, for the chief superintendent was so taken aback that he was unable to reply. Crow took the opportunity presented and rose.

'Furthermore, you mentioned the question of priorities. In fact, I would imagine that for a week or so it's the Lendon case that can be given some priority: after all, I need hardly tell you it's the first two or three days which count in a murder investigation. Things begin to cool thereafter. You've had two months on the Carson investigation: the needs there are hardly so pressing now: you'll have obtained a large number of statements and so on and you'll be going through these, I have no doubt. So there should be little problem in releasing men to assist me.'

Simpson had recovered himself, and was staring at Crow from beneath lowered eyebrows. There was an unpleasant twist to his thick lips. 'I have an idea that we're not going to get on, Inspector Crow.'

'A similar thought had crossed my mind,' Crow said coolly, 'but I was sufficiently inhibited to deny myself the pleasure of saying it, sir. However, I'll take up no more of your time. I called in only at the chief constable's request, to pay my respects.'

'Assume them duly paid,' Simpson replied.

As Crow neared the door Simpson added sarcastically: 'You will, of course, have the courtesy to keep me informed of developments?'

'In so far as they affect you, yes, sir.'

As the door closed behind him Crow cursed under his breath. He had handled the whole thing badly. It was stupid to cross Simpson in that way: Crow had seen the danger signals immediately he'd met the chief superintendent and should have played the whole thing more coolly. Instead, he had lost his temper and his control. Maybe Simpson wouldn't have realized it, for Crow was aware that few people recognized the signs in him — a mildness, a quiet tone was the prelude to sharp words — but nevertheless Simpson would certainly now be more aggressively against the whole Lendon operation. He would not obstruct: he was too conscientious an officer for that, but Simpson would simply make sure that Crow's path wasn't eased.

In a cold anger against himself Crow made his way across to the room placed at his disposal for the duration of the Lendon enquiry. It was time he got down to some work.

Detective-Sergeant Wilson was in the room, preparing to leave. He had one burly arm in the sleeve of his raincoat. 'I'm just off, sir. I've had a word with the sergeant attached to the scene-of-crime unit. He'll be driving me out to the Old Mill: the unit is still out there now.'

'Good. I shall probably take a look out there myself later. Been in touch with the forensic laboratory yet?'

'Yes, sir. The liaison officer is called Roberts. He'll be making lab facilities available as soon as anything comes in.'

Wilson shrugged into his coat and began to do up the buttons. He was a young officer, and a good one. He had been a constable with Crow, when Crow had first obtained promotion to inspector. It could not be too long before Wilson must be off on his own: Crow had put in two reports on the last two cases which would inevitably mark Wilson out for swift promotion to inspector. A little impetuous . . . maybe so, but a good hard Yorkshire head.

'All right, Wilson. Now I'm going down to Lendon's office first. You've got a man down there?' When Wilson nodded, Crow continued, 'And after I've taken a preliminary look there I'll be off up to Lendon's house in . . . er . . . Kenton Lane, isn't it? Right. If anything turns up, then, it's the office or the house.'

'Fine. I'll be away now, sir — the personal details on Lendon are in that file, by the way.'

After Wilson had gone Crow looked through the file.

The bare details were there - Lendon's war record, his entry into the firm, his politics, his local interests, professionally and socially. Unmarried. Housekeeper . . .

The dossier must have been Simpson's work. Swift and efficient, for Lendon had died in the night, some twelve hours ago. But now Lendon's life must come under Crow's microscope. It was one of the things that he disliked, really, this probing into motivations. He could not deny that it fascinated him, but his very fascination in a sense repelled him. People should not need to have the protective shellac scraped away from their private lives. But it happened. In a murder enquiry it happened.

Unmarried. No children. No relatives, apparently. Would Lendon be mourned? Lawyers often were not . . . the thought lingered with him as the car took him swiftly through the town.

Crow was interested to note that the offices of Lendon, Philips and Barrett lay in the more fashionable area of the town's business community. In his experience, solicitors seemed to prefer the older Victorian premises — or perhaps it was the nature of their kind that they should foregather in musty dwellings. Charles Lendon's firm was in the newer part of Canthorpe's office accommodation, however. Premises probably started in the late thirties and now solidly respectable, all brick and stone instead of the glass and plaster jerry-building that would be going on in the outskirts of Canthorpe.

It would seem that Lendon had had the ability to choose well with his employees too. During the course of the afternoon Crow spoke with each of the staff briefly: they were a youthful lot, on the whole. The two assistant solicitors seemed a bright young pair, if a bit callow, particularly the rotund one; the blonde in reception had a giggling fit while he spoke to her but he didn't mind that; the legal executives seemed a conscientious, hard-working group. Philips, the ex-partner, had already called at headquarters and Crow would have to have another word with him later, but it was the articled clerk in whom he became particularly interested.

Cathy Tennant.

She interested him for several reasons. First, there was her direct appraisal of his physical characteristics: she looked him over, noted his appearance and then dismissed it. It was, he realized, of no relevance to her opinions. He was pleased about that: like her, he believed in reaching decisions about people that were uninfluenced by their personal appearance. *Her* personal appearance of course was not against her. She was, he observed, a little on the small side in height, but her figure was a balanced one, and her face a neat oval. She had expressive eyes — they would occasionally betray her, he felt-and her skin was clear, her smile friendly. Decidedly, an attractive girl.

But Cathy Tennant also interested him in that she seemed particularly aware of her surroundings, of people, of events, of motivations. She would be a useful sounding-board, and possibly informative too. Yet she seemed curiously unable to discuss Charles Lendon. For a while he thought that it betokened some sort of intimacy between herself and the dead man, but he dismissed the thought. Her inhibition had another explanation: he guessed it was that she had been unable to reach personal decisions about Lendon, and now her doubts would perhaps never be resolved.

Altogether, an interesting young creature.

'Now then, Miss Tennant, you'll be as aware as I that in an investigation of this nature it's virtually impossible to say what is or is not important. I've spoken to the others in the office, and now I ask you the two questions I asked them. Can you think of any reason why your principal should have been murdered? Is there any event during the last few weeks which might throw some light on his murder? Before you answer, I should add that we are in one of those unfortunate situations where even gossip must be retailed, for within it may lie grains of truth.'

'I'm sure,' Cathy Tennant said, 'that you will already have been regaled with more than enough gossip about Charles Lendon. Particularly his . . . affairs of the heart.'

Delicately put, thought Crow; certainly far more delicately than Philips and the others had phrased it. But then, perhaps Cathy Tennant's youth still caused her to romanticize matters to some extent. From what he had so far heard, Lendon had possessed little romanticism. Rather, his appetites had been fleshly and considerable in their indulgence.

Martha would have liked that phrase, thought Crow : liked it, and laughed at it. She was a good wife; she always took some of the wind out of him in his more portentous moments.

He collected his thoughts again and regarded the girl sitting before him. She was frowning slightly and staring at the floor, her hands still in her lap.

'There *is* something,' Crow suggested.

'Yes.' Her voice was subdued and tinged with reluctance. 'I . . . well, I just don't know how important it is but you people must be judges of that, obviously. The fact is, a week ago, on the Friday, I inadvertently overheard Mr Lendon quarrelling with someone in his office. They were both very angry . . .'

Crow listened without interruption while she gave him details of the quarrel. Her small-boned face was serious, yet not lacking in animation, and once more he obtained the impression that she would be a good witness and one able to grasp, hold and produce details in a way many people could not.

'And you've no idea who the person might be — the one Lendon quarrelled with in the office?'

Cathy Tennant shook her head.

'No. Well, that isn't strictly true, because I'm sure that I *do* know who it is, somehow, for the voice had a familiar ring; yet I just couldn't place it at the time. It might come back to me.'

Crow smiled slightly, and shifted his long legs.

'We must just hope that it does. Good. Now you say that you overheard the quarrel, and then this man left. Did anything else occur that afternoon — did you see Lendon again?'

Again the girl nodded, and Crow was quick to notice the side-slipping glance, the lowering of her eyelids. He was aware that she was reluctant to give him the next piece of information; he suspected that the reluctance was born of sympathy for the person involved.

'Mr Lendon also had an argument with a man called Carson. They . . . they almost came to blows.'

As he listened to her account of the interview between Lendon and Carson that Friday afternoon a week earlier, Crow realized why the girl was reluctant, realized why she desired to utter no condemnation of Carson. The man had lost his treasured daughter; in some way he felt that Lendon had been responsible for that loss, and from Lendon he had received nothing but opposition. But the spasm of sympathy that shot through Crow himself at the image presented by the distraught Carson in Cathy's account did little to inhibit his decision that this was a line he would have to follow up. Miss Tennant knew that as well as he did, and it accounted for her hesitation: she saw as clearly as he that Carson's conduct last Friday might well have some bearing upon the discovery of Lendon's body at Insterley.

'You've been most helpful, Miss Tennant,' Crow said with quiet emphasis. 'I'm much impressed by your clarity and I trust you'll have no objection if I ask you once more. Apart from these two incidents that you mention, was there anything else which might have a bearing upon Lendon's death? Any problems in the office, or with clients, that you are aware of? Did Lendon have any enemies? Is there anyone against whom he might have nursed a grudge, or who might have had cause to dislike him? I repeat, any line you can give us, however slight, might be of the greatest use.'

She hesitated for a moment and then slowly shook her head. At her denial Crow felt something cold move in his stomach. It was an experience he hated, but it was not new to him. It came of a conviction that a person whom he had begun to respect was holding something back from him. And on this occasion, it came to him with regard to Cathy Tennant. He liked her, for her features, her honesty, her clear, expressive eyes. But those eyes had not met his when she had said there was no further information she could impart.

Crow stared at her lowered head. It was a situation he always felt he was ill-equipped to handle, yet it was one which he came across from time to time. It was symptomatic of the regard that he had for people, all kinds of people; he respected their feelings, tried to understand their motives, accepted their desires to hide unpalatable truths. But it was his job to draw out the truth, whether it might hurt or not. It was a part of the job that he hated.

And he would have to do it with this young girl. But not now.

Crow took a quick look around Lendon's room before he left the offices. Detective-Sergeant Turner was already there, looking through the drawers of Lendon's desk.

'Have you checked his appointments book?'

'Yes, sir, I've been making notes of all the appointments he's made of recent weeks, but there are a number of blank spaces which—'

'All right, you can let me have a rundown of the general picture later. There'll be someone on duty here at the office tonight?'

'Yes, sir. Constable Pitt will be here.'

'Make sure the door to this room is locked. I don't want anything in here disturbed.'

As he turned to leave the room Crow noticed the heavy filing cabinet just inside the door. He tried the top drawer. It was locked.

'No sign of the keys yet, sir.'

'They're probably among his effects. Get them up here as soon as possible and get this cabinet opened. What about the anteroom over there?'

'There's a cabinet in there too, but again it's locked.'

'Same thing applies, Turner. I'm away now to the Old Mill. If I'm wanted I can be contacted there this afternoon.'

Chapter 7

In the fading afternoon light the tree-lined track that led up to the Old Mill looked cold and uninviting, rutted with car wheels, and rendered stark by the bare-armed alder and mountain ash, but Crow could imagine that during the summer months the track would certainly be a pleasant one to walk along. He had gathered that the area was regarded locally as something of a lovers' trysting-place and in a sense this was borne out by the number of spaces churned out by parked cars on the sides, under the trees. Crow suspected that couples would make use of the track both in summer and winter, but he equally well knew that although there could be a courting couple who might be able to help in their enquiries, the chances of finding such a couple were not great: young people were reluctant to disclose their courting habits, even when a murder investigation was on hand. And, of course, some of the relevant couples would not want the fact of their courtship to come to light.

The track had left the main road through Insterley some fifty yards below, and about another sixty twisting yards ran ahead through the trees to the Old Mill. The mill proved to be the remains of an old granary, where possibly great wooden arms had once provided the motive power to grind the wheat, but it had been converted into living accommodation at least fifty years ago, and was now uninhabited, its stone decaying, weather-beaten and yellow. The roof had fallen in and the whole structure presented a morose appearance, sullen at the lack of attention paid to it by modern society. Yet it possessed an old-world charm too, a charm that saved it from ugliness and still made it an acceptable meeting-place in whose shadows young lovers could find solitude.

But one man had found only death.

As Crow got out of the car Detective-Sergeant Wilson left the small group of constables engaged in searching the area in front of the mill and approached the chief inspector.

'Anything yet?' Crow asked.

'I'm afraid not, sir. Perhaps you'd like to have a glance inside at the scene, but though there are a few signs of someone having waited there it doesn't look as though there could have been much of a scuffle.'

Crow followed the burly figure of the sergeant into the ruined mill. Wilson pointed to the entrance leading into the inner room on the ground floor.

'The body was found just here. It was lying face forward, with the knees drawn up, the trunk twisted, the face down on the ground.'

'And no scuffle, you say. Does that mean that he might have been meeting someone here that he knew?'

'I imagine he must have made some sort of assignation. After all, why else would he come here? And as to his knowing the killer, well, whether he did or not, it seems to me that it could all have been a matter of surprise. He was lying here in the doorway, sir. It would have been relatively easy for someone to stand just here, behind the wall of the door-frame, and step out with the weapon as Lendon approached. The skewer could have pierced his heart almost before he was aware that there was anyone in the mill.'

Crow stared thoughtfully at Wilson's broad face. The detective-sergeant was not a fanciful man: he tended to be direct in his remarks, and he aired his prejudices and his beliefs in a refreshing way for he recognized them as such, and was not afraid to have them attacked. Crow nodded.

'You used the word "assignation", Wilson. You think he might have been meeting a woman?'

'I understand he was something of a womanizer, sir. This is a spot well known to courting couples.'

'Could a woman have driven that skewer in?'

'I think the pathologists will say that considerable force was used, but that it wouldn't be beyond a woman.'

'And if it wasn't done by a woman, you think that a woman was somehow involved. Lendon was killed by a rival, you think?'

'Possible, sir.'

'We're moving too fast, Sergeant. You've reached conclusions about Charles Lendon's character and you're letting them lead you by the nose.'

'It's one of my failings, sir,' replied Wilson stolidly and without offence. Without glancing at him, Crow knew that there would be a twinkle in his eye.

'Anyway,' Crow continued, it looks as though the blow was delivered swiftly, then—'

'And he died quickly. He fell forward, perhaps against his assailant, and on to his knees. Then forward on to his face, twisting slightly.'

'The killer didn't bother to remove the weapon.'

'That could have been panic, or it could have been deliberate. I doubt whether we'll gain much from our possession of the weapon. Old, rusty, probably picked up in here.'

'You sound pessimistic, Wilson.'

'It's another of my failings, sir.'

Crow stared moodily at the floor. His back was beginning to ache. Tall thin people had weak backs, he'd once heard. He himself had never had any trouble until recently, and that was due to a stupid lifting of a bag of plaster left behind by workmen at his home. It had cost him a slipped disc and three weeks off work. It had cost his colleagues on the murder squad extra duty. But it had meant that there had been three weeks when Martha had not needed to keep a bag packed in the hall, ready for the urgent call to the next assignment.

'By the way, sir, this is Roberts. . .liaison officer with the lab people.' Crow shook hands with the short, stocky sergeant.

'Did the scene-of-crime unit pick up anything with Chief Superintendent Simpson's preliminary investigation?' asked Crow.

Roberts shook his head positively.

'No, sir. The super just sealed off the area, really, and got things sorted out ready for your arrival.'

There was that in Simpson's favour at least, thought Crow. Touchy he might have been, but he didn't meddle. Roberts seemed eager to speak and Crow raised his bushy eyebrows.

'I just wonder whether the lab boys might not come out and have a scrape around as well, sir. The super didn't suggest it, but—'

'Why do you think it a good idea?' Crow's voice was gentle.

'Well, they're scientists, after all, and they might pick up something which we'd miss, sir.'

'How long have you been on liaison, Roberts?'

'Two months, sir.'

Crow nodded.

'Well, take it from me, Roberts, if anyone will find anything here it'll be your colleagues on the force. They're not trained scientists, but they are trained to use their eyes. If you're asking for my view, a lab man is wasting his time coming out with a scene-of-crime unit. He's in the lab to evaluate what we bring him. He's no more capable of finding useful evidence in the first instance than we are — perhaps less so. We find the evidence, he gives us an opinion. It's better that way.'

Roberts seemed a little crestfallen. Crow could not help that. He paced towards the entrance, stooping instinctively as he came out of the Mill even though the high doorway in no sense threatened his tall sparse frame and domed head. It was a matter of habit.

'I'm pushing off now, Wilson, and leaving you to it. I'll see you back at the hotel at nine tonight, and we'll have a short conference, unless anything turns up in the meanwhile, of course.'

'Where will I find you if you are required, sir?'

'In the first instance,' Crow replied sombrely, 'at Charles Lendon's house. I understand he had a housekeeper. I must have a word with her. Later, I'll be in the office, until nine.'

The constable driving the car climbed in behind the wheel and Crow settled himself against the cushions in the rear seat with a sigh. His back was easier now. They jolted their way out of the lane and Crow asked the driver to detail the route to him as they drove towards Lendon's house. It proved to be no more than a mile and a half distant. Lendon must have walked from his home to the Old Mill.

It was another thought worth considering.

'This is Kenton Lane, sir,' said the driver. 'Another twenty yards and we turn off into Woodrow Lane, which is a tarmac track but leads only to Mr Lendon's home, really. It's a private road.'

'I gather that its privacy has been disputed.'

'That's right, sir. Especially since little Jenny Carson was murdered, there's been quite a fuss about it. But Mr Lendon stuck to his guns, as far as I can make out.'

Crow was tempted to pursue the matter, but thought better of it as they were already into Woodrow Lane now. To their right a high beech hedge partly obscured the huddle of council houses that seemed to stretch across the whole area; to the left a skin of silver birch leanly screened patches of dense conifer interspersed with thick bushes of rhododendron. It was a small wood he was looking at, and quiet — yet not so small, either, he realized, as the car slid into the curving drive in front of Lendon's house, and he saw the woods encircling the house and rising thickly against the hill beyond.

'All this didn't belong to Lendon?'

'Oh no, sir. Just the private road and a small area to one side. I think it's owned by a forestry company in London.'

Crow grunted, and eased his spindly legs out of the car.

He took care that his head was not scarred by the top of the door. In his eagerness on his first major case he had entered the station with blood running down his face from a scalp wound. It was not an experience he wished to repeat: he had had every sympathy with the desk sergeant who had goggled unreservedly at the sight of the tall spidery man with a bare, bloodstained skull.

As he crunched across the drive Crow gestured to the constable that he should join him. He rang the doorbell and then stepped back to survey the house. It was surprisingly unpretentious for such a setting: solid, square-built, lead-paned windows, oak and glass door, garage to one side, crazy-paved pathway, long lawns running into the darkness of the woods. Crow had seen better. He had seen worse, too. He glanced briefly at the old Ford that was parked in front of the garage and guessed that it would hardly be Charles Lendon's car. It would never have gone with his image.

The door opened.

The man who faced John Crow was slightly built, of medium height, and nervous. Crow had long ago learned to discount nervousness in a man facing the police — it was usually an unreasoning nervousness.

'You police? We've been expecting you.'

'I'm Chief Inspector Crow.'

'My name's Barnes . . . but it's my sister you'll want to see.'

The little man took a deep breath, controlling himself, and smiled slightly. He led the way through the hall to the sitting-room.

'The police, Alex. Inspector Crow.'

The room was dark, the curtains were drawn and one table-lamp served to light the room only inadequately. The room was as still as a painting and as quiet, but he was hardly aware of it as he looked at Mrs Alexandra Bell. Almost instinctively he glanced back to Barnes for it was difficult to believe that these two were brother and sister. Barnes was thin, but this woman was tall and built upon handsome matronly lines. Barnes's clothes were neat enough but a little shabby; her dress was plain, dignified and uncreased. She shook hands with Crow and it was a firm hand belonging to a decisive woman, a woman of strength. Barnes gave an overall impression of self-effacement and indecision.

Alex Bell's features were composed, her eyes veiled with dark lashes and Crow approved of the clean lines of her face, the straightness of her nose, the warm, full curve of her lower lip. She would have been a lovely girl; she made a handsome woman. She had been Charles Lendon's housekeeper . . . Crow could not help wondering whether their relationship had been closer.

Barnes left them alone.

'I've expected you all day, Inspector.'

Her voice had a rich depth. Her eyes, he now saw, were blue. She was in her early forties.

'How long were you Mr Lendon's housekeeper?' He sensed the slight flinching at the past tense, and yet he could have sworn that she was not a woman given to such weakness.

'Almost ten years.'

'And the last time you saw him?'

'The night he died.'

Crow breathed out slowly.

'Perhaps you'd be good enough to tell me about it.'

Mrs Bell sat with her hands in her lap. Her face was slightly averted; unusual John Crow's appearance might be, but, he suspected, Mrs Bell was a woman to take full advantage of her femininity, and the position she took up was to emphasize the regularity of her profile rather than to avoid looking at his unprepossessing skull.

'There's little to tell, really. He usually arrived back here between five and six. He was a little later that night but not unusually so. I had his evening meal ready for him about eight, as usual—'

She broke off, hesitating, then went on: 'I live up above. There's a small self-contained flat that Mr Lendon had constructed up there. I've lived in the flat for seven years. Each evening he required it I made him a meal. I did on that evening. After he'd eaten, he went out. I never saw him again.'

Patiently, Crow asked: 'Can you provide me with more detail? I mean, how did he seem to you? What did you talk about? Did he say where he was going? Were you not aware of the fact of his non-return?'

Mrs Bell was helpful in her precision.

'When he came home he seemed disinclined to talk. I was aware of a certain edginess in his manner; he seemed anxious about something, worried. As to what we talked about, well, I'll be frank. We quarrelled. Violently.'

Crow regarded the woman facing him in the dimly-lit room and was again aware of the clean, undisturbed line of her profile. She was not afraid to tell him that she and

Lendon had quarrelled. She was a woman of some confidence, and power, and repose.

'What was it about?'

She shrugged, glancing quickly in Crow's direction.

'I can't even remember how it started. I think the whole thing was born of his anxiety, of the worry that he had on his mind. I don't know what it was, but something was upsetting him. Anyway, we started to quarrel and he . . . he said that it was time that I learned my place. I told him in no uncertain terms what I thought my place was. He laughed at me at that, and I completely lost my temper and I slapped him. I went upstairs. Shortly afterwards I heard him leave the house. I made no enquiry as to where he was going. I fell asleep on my bed, and didn't wake until about three in the morning. I then undressed and went to bed, assuming that Charles . . . Mr Lendon had returned in the meanwhile.'

Her voice died away, somewhat theatrically. With some care, Crow framed his next question.

'You will excuse me, Mrs Bell, but you talk of a quarrel, and of slapping him. Your relationship seems to have been . . . odd, for a housekeeper and an employer. You said that you told him what your place should be. What was that, Mrs Bell?'

She understood the significance of the question completely; her head came up and she looked him straight in the eyes. Her hair was dark, but he suspected it would display a russet tinge in the sunlight.

'Charles Lendon should have married me seven years ago. He never did, but he should have done.'

'You were lovers,' Crow said flatly.

'For seven years. When he established the flat here for me. He . . . he made promises.'

'Of marriage?'

She shook her head.

'No. He never said he'd marry me. He was honest in that. But he should have done. His method of seduction—

' and there was a certain cold irony in her voice—'was much more realistic. He offered me security in my widowhood, and he said that after he died I would be provided for. This house, for instance . . .'

Again those eyes held Crow's with a level frankness.

'You must realize that I was a widow, and my brother was . . . not well, and I had very little money. Moreover, Charles Lendon was an attractive man.'

Crow nodded acceptance and understanding. It was not his business how Lendon had conducted his life or his affairs, nor how Mrs Bell had assured her future. He was interested only in Lendon's death, and the circumstances surrounding it.

'Does your brother live here too?'

He sensed a certain reluctance in her, a protective reluctance which was borne out by her tone when she replied.

'No. He visits me regularly, drives out perhaps three times a week. That's his car outside. He suffers from nervous tension and is an out-patient in Canthorpe and a voluntary patient at the Linwood Convalescent Home. He . . . he has had an unhappy life. I am all he has. It was partly because of him that I accepted Charles's suggestion . . .'

Crow was a little surprised at the tremor in her voice.

He had been impressed by her self-sufficiency, her control, her grasp of her emotions, but it was obvious that her relationship with her brother was a protective and deeply emotional one. Crow rose awkwardly to his feet.

'I should like to have a word with your brother in a moment, Mrs Bell. But there are just two more things I want to ask you. First, you were aware of Charles Lendon's reputation?'

She almost smiled.

'I was. Very much so. I take it, from the look on your face, that you are suggesting I might have resented his affairs. You forget, Inspector, I was his housekeeper. We were lovers, true, but it was a business arrangement. I do not pretend I was not fond of him, and I do not pretend I did not obtain some satisfaction from the fact that in spite of his affairs he always returned to me: I was a permanency, while the others were . . . ephemeral. But I knew of his affairs and they were little more than an irritation. No more than that. I was sure of my . . . place, as he called it.'

She was a very cool and self-possessed woman and one quite outside Crow's experience. 'My second question is the obvious one, do you have any idea who might have killed him?'

'A solicitor makes enemies. A man who allows his sexual drive to overrule his discretion makes more. There were many who disliked Charles, many in Canthorpe. On the other hand, I know of none whose dislike was so positive as to lead to murder.'

She pronounced the last word without turning a hair.

Whatever her relationship with Lendon had meant to her over the years, it was perfectly obvious that it had left no wounding emotion, no deep sense of loss in her breast. It became apparent as Crow continued to question her, probing more closely for detail. Alexandra Bell was an intensely practical woman, remarkable for her firm grasp of life and its problems. Perhaps this was what an early widowhood had done for her.

'I'll be sending a man around this evening to go through all Lendon's possessions in the house. You will, of course, leave them untouched.'

'I have my flat.' There was a certain touch of pride in her reply.

'Will your brother stay here with you?' She inclined her head.

'Did Lendon like him?'

'Charles,' Mrs Bell replied with complete honesty, 'disliked John intensely and John was afraid of him. John only came here when Charles was out: he always rang first.'

'And the night Lendon died?'

'John stayed at Linwood, the Canthorpe nursing home, after ringing me earlier. He didn't come near the house, or Kenton Wood.'

Barnes confirmed her remarks a few minutes later when Crow spoke to him in the kitchen. The man had overcome his nervousness now and seemed quite at ease, apart from an inability to hold Crow's gaze directly. Crow remembered Mrs Bell's remark about Barnes's nervous condition.

'So you didn't call here that night?'

'No. I rang my sister and she said Lendon would be home for dinner so I didn't come out. I took a short run in the car up on the London road, but I went back to Linwood fairly early, about eight, and had my usual nightly chat with the porter at the lodge.'

'You and Lendon didn't get on?'

Barnes laughed and shook his head.

'He didn't like me. He didn't want me to come to see Alex so I didn't come when he was here. But I didn't hold it against him. It was his house, after all.'

There was now a certain insouciance in his manner that surprised Crow. Lendon's death had obviously not affected Barnes, but that was hardly surprising since they had not been friendly. Nevertheless, there was an odd confidence in his manner that disturbed Crow. It was the confidence of a man who knew he could in no way assist the police with their enquiries because he had no information to give. . . but paradoxically such people, in Crow's experience, rarely displayed such confidence. They were often the ones who were hesitant.

Crow heard a sound at his back and glanced over his shoulder. A shadow passed from the clouded glass of the kitchen door; Mrs Bell had been standing there, hovering like a disturbed, overprotective mother hen. Crow rose to go but Barnes said casually:

'I hope you're not going to bother Alex too much, Inspector.'

'As little as possible, I assure you. We hope to get the whole thing cleared up quickly.'

Barnes nodded and stood up.

'Besides,' he said in an off-handed manner, 'there are other people you could talk to more profitably than us.'

Crow paused with one bony hand on the door handle. 'What do you mean by that?'

Barnes shrugged and failed to meet Crow's eye. 'Well, Lendon, he had women . . . some of them were married, you know, and then there's Carson . . .'

'What about Carson?'

Barnes licked his lips and hesitated, then rubbed his hands against his sides. A little of his nervousness seemed to have returned.

'Well . . . Carson . . . you must know already what he's been saying publicly about Lendon. You must know he even went to Lendon's office and had a row with him. Alex was telling me that Lendon was furious about it. It wasn't the first quarrel, of course; there was bad blood between them.'

'Why?'

'Jenny, of course. Jenny Carson. She was murdered in the woods, up there.' Barnes gestured out through the kitchen window towards the skyline beyond the house. 'There's a path up there which leads through the wood as a sort of short cut. Children from the council estate play in the woods and if they're late for school, they use the short cut. Carson reckoned, and rightly, that they wouldn't need to take the short cut, not along that path at all if only Lendon would allow them to use Woodrow Lane. But Lendon wouldn't, and someone up there caught Jenny Carson and . . . killed her.'

The little man took a deep breath. His eyes were fixed on the quiet trees, still against the evening sky.

'Carson's been after Lendon ever since, to open that right of way. I think you ought to see Carson. I think it was Carson who could have killed Charles Lendon. Ask him where he was when Lendon died. Ask him if he killed Lendon for revenge. Ask him . . .'

Barnes suddenly seemed hardly aware of Crow. His voice dropped until it was little more than a whisper.

'It was a cold dry night when they found her. Frosty. It had been that way for days. Maybe that was why the police haven't been able to find much to help them, because hard ground doesn't show much. And she was such a little girl, she couldn't have done much to fight him off, fight off that man who killed her. We all helped to search, we all came beating through the woods and it was Edwards from Hamberley who came across her in the end. Her face was all black somehow we couldn't understand that but it was the dirt and the terror and the throttling hands. She'd been dragged under some bushes and there were long scratches down her arms and along her legs and her left ankle was broken and her tongue was almost bitten through. They said she must have tried to scream and he'd jammed a hand under her chin and teeth and they must have almost severed her tongue with the force . . .'

Crow listened with mounting distaste. Barnes had taken part in the search, he must have seen the body, probably gone to the inquest, listened with an avid, fearful fascination to every detail of the girl's death and now it was as though he was not talking about a little girl at all — he was using the expressionless tones of a police surgeon.

There was something of the ghoul about John Barnes. But the man was right, Crow thought, as the car turned into Woodrow Lane towards the council estate. He would have to pay a visit to Carson. Other thoughts flickered into his mind: Alexandra Bell, a calm, controlled woman, a splendid woman in so many ways, and yet there was a calculation about her, an iron in her character that made him feel she'd stop at little to achieve her own ends. He thought of her, and the timetable of Lendon's movements the day he died, his reason for visiting the Old Mill, the question as to why he'd walked rather than driven. Then there were the files in the office, the quarrel overheard by Cathy Tennant. He wondered briefly whether he ought to have a word with Chief Superintendent Simpson about Barnes, for he felt that something about the man did not ring true. He shrugged the thought aside: the Carson case wasn't his business, he had to look at all these other pieces, the small, unconnected and perhaps insignificant pieces. Would they fit together, form a pattern of action, a pattern of behaviour?

A pattern for murder?

Chapter 8

After John Crow had left him James Carson walked into the sitting-room and sat in the easy chair. Its arms were badly worn, picked by restless fingers during these last terrible months. It was over these arms Jenny used to clamber to put her chubby arms around his neck, when she was three. From this chair he used to watch her play in the back garden, muddying his freshly planted seeds, trampling the early daffodils in the first excitement of a spring sun.

During those short years she'd been with them he'd seen the glow in her red, winter-livened cheeks, seen the sun in her bright hair and the happiness in her laughing mouth, when she was seven.

He remembered the outing to the cinema when she was eight; when they returned he'd sat in this chair and watched her spread out her books and toys in front of her. Her ninth birthday, now, that had been a laughing time, when Jenny had hugged the enormous teddy-bear that Uncle Jack had brought her from Liverpool, and she'd chased the Terry girls round and round the room in a wild tempestuous game of blind man's bluff. It had been a good birthday, that last one, she'd enjoyed it to the full and he'd thought how he'd always try to make sure that all her birthdays would be enjoyable. She had, of course, behaved as most young children do on such occasions — she'd eaten and eaten, and drunk far too much and had protested that it wasn't time for bed and had fallen asleep even before her father had left the bedroom. He had stood there that October evening, and watched her in the cool darkness, marvelling that sleep could come so quickly, and so rosily, and so happily . . .

But when the final sleep had come it had arrived with a screaming agony and terror, with strange, incomprehensible pain, with a scrabbling and a scrambling, harsh breathing, heavy, hard hands that had shown none of her mother's gentleness or her father's love. There could have been only the fearful darkness and the weight, the blood and the tearing bushes and the hard ground and the frantic, frantic beating of a terrified child's heart.

The thought brought the moan rising in Carson's throat again as it always did when his mind lurched back despairingly in this way; the rising, agonized pain in his chest that all but stilled his breathing, the rasp in his lungs, the tumultuous racing beat of his pulse, as the memories and the indescribable loss and the love smothered him and demanded tears.

But no tears came.

They had not come that night, when Edwards had shouted, far across to his left. They had not come when James Carson had blundered his way through the bushes, throwing aside the restraining arms like an enraged bull. They had not come when he stared down at the torn body of little Jenny, neither then, nor at the inquest nor at the funeral. Nor now, nor on any of the long dark nights.

He felt a hand on his shoulder. Carson shuddered, focused his eyes and looked over the back of the chair. Marion stood there with her ravaged face still lashed with incomprehension. She had seen him sitting here like this so many times these last months, and he knew that she felt an immense distress at being unable to help him. Perhaps a wife should be able to help a husband, perhaps he should be able to accept her help. But it wasn't that easy. This chair, everything in the house . . . Jenny . . .

'When is it going to end, Jim?' Marion asked suddenly. She was forty-three now but her hair was greying and her light prettiness was lined and savaged as his heart had been by Jenny's death. He could not reply to her and simply shook his head. But he sat up in the chair, and tried to wash everything away, for her sake as much as for his own.

She handed him the cup of cocoa that she customarily made at this time and he felt her hesitation as she took the chair opposite him, in front of the fire. At last she asked the question he had been expecting.

'The chief inspector was here a long time. What did he really want, Jim? It wasn't about Jenny, was it?'

Carson shook his heavy hand and sipped at the hot cocoa before he answered. 'No. Not about Jenny.'

'Then it was about Mr Lendon, wasn't it? What did the inspector want, Jim? Why did he come here?'

He sensed and understood the current of fear in her tone and did his best to lull the quick panic that would be rising in her.

'It's all right, Marion. There's nothing to worry about. He was just checking, that's all. You see, I went down to Lendon's office a week ago to . . . to argue the case about the lane again. We had . . . we had a bit of a scuffle and Miss Tennant was there and saw it and I suppose she had to tell the police, but that's all there was to it. He was just checking, that's all. Just checking.'

Marion was silent, staring into the fire. Her hands were wrapped around her cocoa cup as though for warmth, but the room was warm.

'He's an ugly man, isn't he,' she said. 'I mean, he's so tall, and his head is such a funny shape. He's like a skeleton.' She blushed in confusion even as the words came out, as though she wished they had not been spoken. She looked at him anxiously.

'But there's something about him, Jim, isn't there. . .didn't you feel it? He wouldn't *do* anything to us, would he? You know what I mean, he was sort of . . . nice, wasn't he? He wouldn't *do* anything to us, not after Jenny was . . .'

Carson leant forward and touched her hand with a gentleness surprising in such a large man.

'There's nothing he can do to us, Marion. Believe me, there's nothing he can do.'

'Oh Jim—'

Doubt still struggled with the hope in her eyes, but after a moment she sat back quietly and continued to stare into the fire. They did not speak again until twenty minutes had elapsed and the two cocoa cups lay empty.

'Time for bed, Marion,' Carson said gently. He saw the pain in her face but stubbornly, insistently ignored it. She nodded, and rose with reluctance. As she walked past the chair her hand touched his shoulder again.

'Jim.' Her voice was quiet and pleading. 'Will you . . . will you come to me tonight? Please?'

He put his large hand over hers, tenderly, but did not look up to her.

'No, girl, it's better the way it is. You go to your room. You sleep, get your strength up. I'll not disturb you.'

'Jim—' she began, but subsided as the pressure of his hand on hers increased. He knew she was near to tears but he could not do as she asked. Her hand slipped away, and she walked to the door. She stopped, reluctantly.

'When he was here. . .that policeman. Did he ask you if you were at home the night that Mr Lendon died?'

Carson's hands were still. In the silent room there was only the crackle of the fire to suggest life. He did not answer her, but slowly countered her question with one of his own.

'Did he ask *you* that question, Marion?'

'Yes,' she replied in a whisper.

'And you told him?'

The answer was a long time coming.

'I . . . I said to him that you were here . . . with me. Oh, Jim. . .'

He shook his head, and rose slowly, but stubbornly. 'I've told you, Marion,' he said, as he began to remove his slippers. 'I've told you. There is nothing that policeman can do to us.' Slowly, he reached for his boots.

* * *

Two hours later Constable Pitt decided to make himself a cup of tea. His orders were to remain on post at the entrance to the offices of Lendon, Philips and Barrett, but it was a cold, miserable night and he was pretty certain that no one would be along to check on him tonight. And he'd seen a gas-burner in the small office on the ground floor where the typists made tea for themselves. Quietly he let himself into the offices, using the key Sergeant Turner had given him.

He thought it best not to turn on the lights. He used his flash lamp to make his way to the gas-burner, then he put the lamp down, took off his helmet and loosened his coat, lit the gas-burner and waited for the kettle to boil. Nice kids, those typists, leaving a full kettle for him!

He began to whistle through his teeth, a low, tuneless noise that drove his colleagues to desperation when they were in earshot. He was all alone now.

He made the tea, poured a cupful and added milk and sugar from the basins he found in the cupboard. Home from home. He sat in the semi-darkness and listened to the creaks of the old building. Funny how boards and stairs creaked like that, it was the same in the terrace house in Manchester where he'd lived as a boy. Always noises at night.

But not thudding. Not a regular, low, monotonous thudding. The muffled sound of a window banging, there

70

was one like that in Edith's room back home, always banging in the middle of the night.

Constable Pitt picked up his flashlight, put down his cup and walked into the hallway, up the stairs to the first floor and started looking for the open window. He found it within minutes, but was puzzled to discover that the catch was broken. He closed the window and put down the lamp so that he could use both hands to secure the window. He began to whistle again, in the same tuneless tone.

It was only at the last moment he heard the swift step behind him.

He half turned and saw the dark figure but it was already too late. In the dimness an arm was sweeping down towards his unprotected head. He'd left his helmet downstairs. Even as he staggered back under the blow his thoughts were logical.

There'll be hell to pay about this, he thought.

Chapter 9

'I gather you played hell,' Crow said quietly and stared around at Lendon's room.

Wilson grunted sourly. 'What I had to say didn't help his sore head, sir.'

'Mmm. Well, there's nothing we can do about it now it's happened. What've you got to report?'

'Pitt heard a noise, came up to investigate, got hit on the head with this portable dictating machine.'

Crow took the machine from him and inspected it critically.

'It won't be much use now. Pitt must have a hard head. Any prints on it?'

'Wiped clean, sir.'

'How did the intruder get in?'

'There's a window on the first floor that was forced open. Six feet below the window is a sloping roof: an easy climb from the top of dustbins at the back. He must have entered when Pitt was at the front and Pitt disturbed him when he came upstairs.'

'And he'd entered this room. The lock was forced, I see. All right, better tell me the worst. What's been taken?'

Wilson scratched his head.

'Difficult to say. Very little, I suspect, sir. The papers on the table are still more or less as they were, according to Turner. But the lock on this cabinet here has been broken, and it's my guess that some of the files may have been taken.'

Crow took out some files from the top drawer and riffled through them. They were all headed with individual names, and seemed to be colour-coded, but there was no immediate clue as to what the code meant.

'When did Pitt raise the alarm?'

'About two-thirty a.m. He was a bit concussed till then. I took the call and saw no reason to disturb you at once, sir. The details were a matter of routine, so I just went ahead.'

'You're concerned about my beauty sleep, obviously,' Crow said and Wilson permitted himself a tight smile. 'All right, we'll—'

'Excuse me, sir.'

The young, fresh-faced constable who had entered the room shuffled nervously. 'The first of the office staff has arrived. A Miss Tennant. Should she be allowed to her room?'

'Oh yes, there's no reason why she should get in our way. She works on the. . .wait a minute.' Crow paused, reflecting. 'Ask her if she'll come up here for a moment.'

Two minutes later Cathy Tennant was facing Crow. 'You're in early this morning, Miss Tennant.'

Her eyes displayed surprise at the activity in the building.

'I woke early, couldn't get back to sleep. What's . . . what's happened?'

'An intruder during the night. We think some files might have been taken. Lendon used a colour code. It occurs to me that you might know its significance.'

She shook her head. Now that Crow had had time to look at her he realized that there were dark rings around her eyes; he suspected she had slept little last night. For a moment he wondered whether he should question her again, attempt to worm out of her the extra information he was sure she was keeping back from him, but he decided against it. She wasn't sleeping well; perhaps time would eat away at her resolve in this way, disturb her conscience until she told him everything. He had other things to do, and the girl might come to her senses without his badgering.

'Was anything taken from the other cabinet?' she asked suddenly.

'The other one?'

'In the anteroom.'

She showed it to Crow; it was locked and when he put his bony shoulder against it the weight of it suggested that it was pretty full of papers.

'Keys?'

'I think Turner's got Lendon's keys now . . . picked them up last night from the lab.'

'Well, I want this opened at once.'

'Perhaps my keys will open it,' Cathy said and opened her handbag. 'The office equipment is pretty standard and they'll probably fit. Here, let's try this one.'

She inserted a key, and then exclaimed in triumph as the locking device slid back. She pulled the top drawer open with a flourish. 'There you are!'

'That's most helpful of you, Miss Tennant. Now if you—'

'Turner's arrived, sir.'

Wilson's remark caused Crow to break off and turn around. He and Wilson moved away from the cabinet to speak to Turner and collect the missing keys from him, asking him whether the lab had any information to date. It wasn't the first mistake that Crow had made in his police career, but it was his first in the Lendon case. It was while he was extending his hand for the keys from Turner that Cathy Tennant stood rigidly staring at the top drawer and the suspended files it contained; it was as he was turning back to the anteroom that Cathy Tennant saw the crumpled note stuffed into the front of the drawer and recognized its signature.

Neither Crow nor Wilson made any attempt to detain Cathy as she made her way downstairs to her office, for neither had any reason to do so. After all, neither of them had observed her swiftly remove the single sheet of paper from the drawer and slip it into the pocket of her coat.

Cathy kept herself busy for the rest of the day and saw no more of the chief inspector or the two sergeants. She was glad of that, for she was agonized with anxiety. She took care that it did not show. Nevertheless, when Chief Inspector Crow came into her room the next day her pulse raced, for she knew Crow to be a man of perception and she was equally aware that she was unused to subterfuge, to dishonesty, to lying.

She guessed that Crow suspected she knew more than she had told him but he hadn't pressed her. This frightened her as much as anything; it was as though Crow felt he could rely upon her innate honesty to tell him the truth, rely upon the sympathy that already existed between them.

She felt that he knew her, and knew her transparency. But he did not know about the paper in the filing cabinet, and she was still appalled at her own temerity in abstracting it. She couldn't yet be certain that she would have the courage to retain it. If he ever suspected . . .

He was smiling at her. Gaunt and unlovely he might be in his general appearance, but he had a nice smile; it had warm edges.

'Still hard at it, Miss Tennant?'

'That's right, Inspector. Mr Parnell and Mr Maxwell are handling things for the time being, and there's plenty to do.'

'I'm sure there is. Er . . . has Sergeant Turner been in?'

'Yes, Inspector. He came in about thirty minutes ago and is in Mr Lendon's room. I imagine he's ploughing through the files.'

'Ahuh. Would you mind buzzing him on the intercom, Miss Tennant, and asking him to come through to join us here?'

Cathy complied with the request. Crow sank into a chair and stretched his long thin legs out in front of him. He ran a hand over his bald skull. His eyes were tired. 'Now then, Miss Tennant, while we're waiting for the sergeant, may I ask you if you've thought of any further points since I spoke to you last?'

'I'm afraid not, Inspector.' There was no tremor in Cathy's voice to match that which shuddered through her veins. But she was not a good liar, and she imagined she read the thought in Crow's sad eyes.

'You've not remembered the voice in the office . . . not thought who it might be yet?'

'I'm afraid not. I lay awake for some time last night, and I kept thinking about it. It's so silly in a sense, for I feel sure that it's someone I know well. It lies in my head, you know, a little muffled as the voice was in the office that day. Like speaking through cotton wool.'

'But it was a voice you ought to recognize?'

'Indeed. It will come back to me.'

There was a light tap on the door and the stocky figure of Detective-Sergeant Turner entered. He sat down at Crow's invitation, and in answer to his superior's question he replied: 'Well, I sorted out most of the files yesterday, as I told you, sir, but there are about thirty of these red files which seem to hold pretty personal material. This is a list of them: they were all contained in the cabinet in the anteroom to Mr Lendon's office.'

Crow looked at her carefully, and Cathy sat still.

'I'll read the list of names to you, Miss Tennant, and perhaps you could tell me if any of them strike significant chords for you . . . you know, people who might have a strong grudge against Lendon.'

'Why me, Inspector Crow? I hardly knew Mr Lendon outside the office!'

'Miss Tennant,' Crow interrupted, 'I'll be frank. You've impressed me as a young woman with some quality of foresight, some honesty, and some clarity of thought. I feel that you knew Lendon better than you yourself even imagine. I feel that you possess a naturally analytical turn of mind that may well have enabled you to see and perhaps understand things that others would overlook. I shall ask Mr Parnell the same questions, in fact, but I ask you now for the reasons I've given. Now, the names . . .'

He read them slowly. There were several that Cathy recognized, but few that meant anything of significance to her.

'No good?' asked Crow.

'Not really.' She hesitated for a moment. 'But there's one name there . . . Charlton, he's dead, you know.'

'Tell me.'

'Oh, he was killed in a road accident about six weeks ago. Hit by a bus, I think. He was a private enquiry agent, in fact, and had been employed once by Mr Lendon.'

'Once?'

'Well, yes, we usually use the Clan Agency, but I met Mr Charlton here in the office and in an attempt to impress me — he wanted a date — he told me that Mr Lendon was employing him. He was from out of town.'

Cathy had already caught the glance that flashed from Crow to Turner and she placed her own interpretation on it: they would be looking closely into the circumstances of the death of Mr Charlton. She doubted whether they'd find anything there, for as she remembered it had been a straightforward accident. She watched as Crow thoughtfully extracted one file from the others and placed it on the top. The lettered heading was upside down to her but she could read it well enough. *Charlton.*

'So there's nothing else?'

'I'm afraid not, Inspector.'

'All right. Now then, that afternoon Lendon had the two quarrels — where did he go?'

'I don't know. Doesn't his appointment book—'

'There's no entry for the period between one and four in the afternoon. Indeed, there are three days during a period of a fortnight when the pages are similarly blank. The third of those days was the afternoon of the day he died.'

'I'm afraid—'

'Where was he on those days, Miss Tennant?'

'I've no idea.'

'Could he have been meeting a woman?'

'Well, I suppose he could have been, but—'

'Where were *you* on those days, Miss Tennant?'

The room was suddenly silent. Cathy felt the blood draining from her face. The implication of Crow's sudden question was like a douche of cold water and, for a moment, she was unable to frame an answer. Then, coldly, and with dignity she said: 'My own appointment book—'

'I checked it last night,' Sergeant Turner said heavily, 'and you've been less than careful in filling it in.'

'When it's blank, it means I'm just working here in the office.'

'We're not implying anything,' Crow said. 'Just checking possibilities.'

'I was here in the office on each of the afternoons.'

'I'm sure you were.'

Crow's sympathetic smile only served to increase her pulse rate. Her own sense of guilt was rising strongly . . . all right, in the first instance she'd just been reluctant to tell him of Mike's dislike for Lendon, but now there was the letter . . . but he couldn't know about that. And she couldn't — daren't — tell him.

'We've gone through the files in both filing cabinets now,' Crow said quietly. 'Our intruder made a bad mistake.

Lendon, it would seem, was a careful man. Two drawers in the cabinet in the anteroom simply contained duplicates of the files in his room. Our intruder took three files, we suspect, from the cabinet in Lendon's room, without realizing that they were duplicated in the anteroom. It looks as though it's going to . . . ah . . . help us with our enquiries. As you can, Miss Tennant, if you will go down to the anteroom in about ten minutes' time.'

When she agreed to do so Crow thanked her and left with Turner. Cathy sat there somewhat puzzled, until she was disturbed by the jangling telephone.

She picked up the receiver and her heart sank. It was the one voice she didn't want to hear, the one person she didn't want to speak to.

'No,' she said, 'I can't make it tonight.' The voice was insistent.

'No, I can't make it, not even later. I have to stay at home and wash my hair and—'

There was anger in the voice now, but again she said she couldn't go out. The caller rang off abruptly. She replaced the receiver with care and sadly walked across to the window. An immense feeling of depression washed over her. She stood staring out across the street but she saw nothing. She saw none of the buses that passed, nor the dark-suited gentlemen. She was hardly aware of the two lorries, the fifteen bicycles, and the thirty-five private cars that drove past during the next six minutes. And she did not see, as she turned away from the window at Detective-Sergeant Turner's invitation, the small blue Volkswagen drive past the entrance to Lendon, Philips and Barrett, and proceed up to the next junction, turn left, and park at the end of the long road that led down to the children's playground and pleasure park. But even had she seen it, Cathy would probably have paid it no attention, for she did not know its occupant.

The woman who got out of the car was thirty years old.

Her face was heart-shaped, her eyes a warm, alluring brown. She possessed a slender figure, but one that displayed her expensive and carefully chosen clothes to advantage. She was not tall, her legs were not long, but she presented overall the sort of picture of womanhood that many men in their mind's eye dreamed of: warm, exciting, passionate and available.

But Mrs Gillian Kent was not available. For more than five years she had been separated from her husband, but she had managed to keep well away from the types of men who quickly sought to turn to their advantage a situation where they felt she must surely need sexual comfort. For five years she had kept free of such men, and for the last eighteen months it had not been too difficult, for her own sexual desires, always a force to be reckoned with, had been assuaged — and this had meant she could present an even colder shoulder to her transient admirers.

This did not mean that she resented their glances, and she was aware of several now as she stepped out of the blue Volkswagen, locked the door and walked quickly down the street. She did not resent them but she ignored them, nevertheless.

She was a little breathless.

When she finally turned into Gethin Road her breathlessness had increased, but she knew it was not due to the speed of her step. She slowed deliberately, and attempted to control her breathing and the pace of her heartbeat. She still walked on, nevertheless, towards the white-painted door to No. 37 Gethin Road.

The receptionist smiled her usual perfect smile and stood up behind her neat, clean-swept desk.

'Good morning, Mrs Kent. Do you wish to make an appointment?'

'Is Dr Barstow in surgery yet?' The smile remained professionally perfect.

'Not for another hour, Mrs Kent. Do you wish to see him before then?'

'If it is at all possible.'

'Well, I'm not sure.' The receptionist looked doubtful letting the smile harden just slightly at the corners to denote that the appointments system was the child of her nurturing and was not to be despised. 'But I'll see.'

She lifted the telephone and waited. Then, with her careful, low-modulated telephone voice she murmured:

'Dr Barstow, Mrs Kent is here and would like to see you if this is not inconvenient.'

There was a pause and the receptionist's eyes lifted to Mrs Kent. The smile was switched on again, briefly. 'You can go in, Mrs Kent. Dr Barstow will be pleased to see you.'

Gillian Kent inclined a graceful head and walked through the door held open for her by the receptionist. She crossed to the door at the far end of the passageway. She tapped at it lightly, heard the intoned command, entered and closed the door behind her. She stood leaning against it, both hands braced, as she stared at Dr Barstow, rising from his chair. His wide eyes held a hint of anger and his jaw was set hard but she didn't care. Deliberately she walked across the room and took him by the shoulders. She kissed him, hungrily, and even though anger stiffened his lips they moved against hers and she felt that nothing had changed for him, it was the same as always, the same as it had been this last eighteen months.

He pulled away from her, with an involuntary glance to the window. There was perspiration on his brow and he twitched at his tie convulsively.

'For God's sake, Gillian, you must be crazy coming here like this! You know what we always said, you know what we arranged.'

'Darling, it's different now.' Her voice was edged with strain and longing. 'It's different now, for we're free.'

'Are you mad? What do you mean-*free*?'

He was looking at her with glaring eyes. There was a nervous tic at the corner of his sensuous mouth, and he ran his fingers across his lips suddenly.

'Darling,' she murmured, 'he's dead. He's dead, and we're free, and the whole filthy, ugly episode can be forgotten and we can be together again, just as we were before.'

Paul Barstow shook his handsome head violently, and turned away. She watched him walk across to the window, saw the anxiety in the set of his broad shoulders and she couldn't understand it, any of it.

'Darling, Lendon's dead and it is all right now, surely!'

He flashed a quick, angry glance at her over his shoulder and shook his head again.

'It isn't all right. I thought at first that it would be changed, but it hasn't, it can't. We're no further forward, we're no better off. And I told you never to come here again, to wait until I rang you, until things were quiet when we could meet out at Rains Point again, as we used to. And now, at the first chance you come charging in here like an empty-headed fool! Don't you realize what you're doing? Don't you realize that this way you can ruin everything? Don't you realize that once people suspect us, see us together, start adding things up, it could be finished between us for good? Hell, the way things stand now we could well be washed up already!'

Gillian Kent stiffened, hardly able to believe her ears.

She stood staring at the man she loved and she could not understand what he was trying to say. Or perhaps she understood him only too well.

'You made me,' she mumbled. 'When Charles Lendon put the pressure on *you,* you came to me, you asked me, you *made* me do it. And now, after I've done what you wanted, now, after he's dead, you say that nothing has changed. You shamed me and humiliated me and now you say we're back where we started. Worse than that, you say that we could be finished. You say that things are dead between us . . . when it was *you* who fixed it that way.'

He rocked his head from side to side in slow denial. 'You don't understand me, Gillian. I'm trying to say you shouldn't have come here, I'm trying to tell you we have to be careful . . .'

'Are you in love with me, Paul?'

Her words leapt across at him like a lash and he flinched. His eyes failed to meet hers, and he made no reply.

'Do you love me?'

Even as he looked at her dumbly she lost control: she crossed the space between them in two strides and struck out at him hysterically. Her right hand caught his cheek a stinging blow but his up-raised arm caught the next blow, deflected it and then his strong arms were round her, pinioning her hands to her side, and his handsome face was close to hers, his breath warm on her cheek.

'Don't be such a damned fool! Listen to me, and think! Think! Lendon is dead, but though I thought at first it would make a difference I realize now that it doesn't. Can't you see that? What will be happening up there now, today, at his office? Lendon is dead, and what was in his head has gone with him, but how do we know he didn't keep records? How do we know that everything was not put down on paper? How do we know that the police are not at this very minute going through his files, and discovering all about this mess?'

Gillian stared at him, wild-eyed.

'Are you . . . are you trying to say that it was all pointless? That in spite of what I did—'

'Lendon's dead,' Barstow said with a snarl, 'but the police will know, or guess. I'm sure of it. And you come here today!'

Slowly her chin came up. She was beginning to see Paul Barstow with new eyes, and she didn't like what she saw. The man was badly frightened.

'I love you, Paul,' she said slowly and with studied care. 'Does it matter, does any of it really matter, if we love each other?'

'Don't be so bloody childish! What the hell is going to happen now God only knows! While it was only Lendon who knew, we stood a chance—'

'Did we? Did we *ever* really stand a chance, Paul, me and you? I'm not sure now, not sure at all.'

'What are you going to do?' he asked in a voice harshened with strain as she turned to go. 'Do? Embarrass you no further. Leave you, accepting that I should never have come. Go back home and sit by the telephone, wait for you to call. But will you ever call? Will you ever call me again?'

A spasm of doubt crossed his face and he put out a hand to her. She ignored it coolly. 'Perhaps I should have guessed that under the strain we've suffered any love you did have would be eroded. I'm no longer the same woman to you, am I, Paul?'

'You don't understand, Gillian. It's not that way. It's just that we have to stay careful, for a while at least, until suspicion dies and then later, maybe we—'

'Yes. Maybe we can. But not now. I'll go home now, Paul, like a good girl. Shall I say goodbye, or leave it at *au revoir?*'

'Gillian—'

She let herself out into the corridor. She knew that he would make no attempt to follow her. She walked carefully out past the receptionist, and managed to smile as she had managed to smile over these last eighteen months. But those months had given her a great deal to smile about: the last few minutes had robbed her of all that. Yet she smiled. Perhaps it was a measure of the way her character had hardened. Perhaps it was a measure of her guilt.

Lendon was dead, but nothing had changed.

A few heads turned as she walked back to the car, though on this occasion she was not aware of them. Tears pricked at the back of her eyelids, but she kept her head up and the watery sun gleamed on her lashes. She reached the Volkswagen, unlocked it, sat behind the driving seat for a few minutes, stiffly, dully, then started the car and drove it carefully from her parking place.

Two minutes later it passed the offices of Lendon, Philips and Barrett, but once again Cathy Tennant did not see the blue Volkswagen. For Cathy was no longer standing at the office window. She was coming out, white-faced, from the anteroom to Charles Lendon's office. She was looking at Chief Inspector Crow and Sergeant Turner and her hand was shaking slightly. Crow was leaning forward, his head thrust out like a great predatory bird.

'Well?' he asked, and there was a note of underlying urgency in his voice. Cathy nodded, in a sad conviction.

'Yes, I recognized it, muffled through the door, as you were talking with him. The man you've been speaking to is the man who was quarrelling with Charles Lendon on that Friday afternoon, the week before Mr Lendon was murdered.'

Chapter 10

Detective-Sergeant Wilson arrived at the operations room to join Crow and Turner, carefully hung his blue raincoat behind the door and took a chair near Crow's desk.

'Well, what have we got?' Crow asked.

Wilson hitched himself forward in his chair and extracted a battered notebook from his pocket.

'I've left two men from the scene-of-crime unit up at the Old Mill; they'll be there for the rest of the day. The others have finished there now. We've more or less cleaned the place out and there's very little to go on. Still, the picture would seem to be fairly clear.'

'That sounds ominous. When a "picture" is clear it usually turns out to be far from the truth.'

'It's as near as we can work it out, anyway, sir. I've checked the statements of the principal witnesses so far and the facts as we know them are these: after leaving his home at eight-thirty or thereabouts Lendon walked up to the Old Mill . . .'

'We still don't know why he didn't take his car.'

'No, sir, we don't.'

Wilson paused as Crow's head sank on to his narrow chest. He knew the signs when Crow would be lost in thought. What he could not know, of course, was that Crow was thinking of Alex Bell and the way the light had caught her russet hair.

'It could be,' Wilson continued, 'that he walked up to the Old Mill simply to ensure that he'd be unobserved; maybe he just wanted no advertisement of his presence. He would have reached the Old Mill, walking briskly, at some time just after nine in the evening. We've found an empty packet of cigarettes, of the expensive kind that he smoked, among the trees just short of the mill, so there's the possibility that he waited there for a little while.'

'Waiting for someone?'

'Or watching for someone . . . who can tell? Anyway, he couldn't have been there long because we found only one cigarette butt there, and that half smoked. It would seem, therefore, that at about nine-fifteen he walked forward to the door of the Old Mill. There are three footprints in soft earth under the trees that may well be his: the lab boys are working on it.'

'And then?'

'It's mainly as I say. He walked into the Old Mill, and prowled around, I guess. Then he stepped forward to the inner doorway. There's nothing to suggest what happened either way thereafter. It's possible that he met the person he came to see and stood talking; it's equally possible that he just walked forward and was attacked.'

'Which do you think happened?' Wilson frowned thoughtfully.

'My impression is that there was no talking, no discussion. There was no sign of a struggle. Now, if you think about it, if we were standing talking and I suddenly produced a skewer and thrust at you, you'd step back, wouldn't you, try to avoid the blow? Well, there's no sign of his stepping back, no scuffing of the thick dust around there. He just came forward on to his face. I think he was still walking forward when that skewer hit him. It doubled him up, forward, and down he went.'

'You think it's likely that he didn't even see his assailant?' Wilson nodded.

'I think someone was waiting there for him, and as he came through the opening in the darkness . . . wham!'

'Very descriptive,' Crow remarked dispassionately. 'But could he not have fallen forward if the blow had been given to him when standing close to someone, when he could not see the weapon to step back? When he was embracing or about to embrace a woman, for instance?'

'*Cherchez la femme.*' Wilson's shrug was expressive. 'It's a line of enquiry that I intend to pursue. We know what Lendon's predilections were; we know that the Old Mill is a lovers' haunt. He could have been going to meet a woman. The question is . . .'

'Who?'

'Precisely.'

Wilson pursed his lips and stared at Sergeant Turner. 'Anything in the files you've been looking at?'

'A great deal,' Turner replied, 'and a lot of it is more than interesting. I haven't finished yet, because we've been mugging up on one file in particular this morning, but so far, no homicidal "birds" appear.'

'Sergeant Turner will keep looking, after the interview we're to mount shortly. Anyway, what we do know is that Lendon was absent from this office on three occasions in two weeks during the afternoons, and there's no record of where he might have been. I think he could possibly have been meeting a woman. It could have been the woman who met him at the mill.'

'If it *was* a woman who met him there,' Wilson said.

Crow smiled pallidly and nodded agreement. One could not really reach such conclusions without proof.

'On the afternoon he died,' Crow continued, 'Lendon was out of the office until four-thirty, as he was a week earlier before his quarrel with Carson. The day he died, he

88

worked here for about an hour or so, then left for home at about six. It would seem that he stopped somewhere on the way, for he was late getting back to the house. He had dinner at eight—'

Wilson leaned forward to interrupt.

'When you say he stopped somewhere, sir, I can tell you where he stopped. It was on a lay-by a mile out of town: it's in Constable Parker's book. He was patrolling in the Panda and passed Lendon's car twice. Took a look at it the second time, wondering what he was doing. Lendon was alone. Just sitting. Appeared not to notice the Panda.'

Crow's eyes were wide with interest. 'Is that so?' He lifted a hand and with long, bony fingers teased and twisted at his lower lip. 'Now why would he just sit there . . . waiting for someone, again? Why would anyone go to a lay-by like that instead of going home, and just sit, alone?'

'Anyway, that's where he was.' Crow nodded with satisfaction.

'That's something, at least. Mrs Bell has said that he appeared worried and edgy. Maybe he just pulled into that lay-by to think things out. What things? Well, we'll see. We'll see what emerges. At least we know he was home later, had dinner at eight, then walked out at eight-thirty.'

'And ended up with a skewer in his heart.'

The room fell silent. Crow's face was expressionless, and Turner glanced across to Wilson, but the sergeant sat passively, staring at Crow, waiting. He was obviously used to Crow's attitudes and postures and way of working. Turner was not, but decided that he would simply follow Wilson's lead in this. He remained silent.

'Good,' Crow said suddenly. 'We'll get on, then. Turner, you will go through the rest of the files apart from the Charlton one, which you'll leave to Wilson. I've looked at it,' he explained to Wilson, 'but there's not a great deal there. I'll want you to check Charlton's own files, and look into the circumstances of the man's death. He was an enquiry agent, employed just once by Lendon. I'll also want you to keep things tied up with the lab people, Wilson, and at HQ. I'll be reading some of these files tonight, before I go out to the Lendon home again. There are two men up there going through his belongings and papers at the house. I want to take a quick look myself.'

Crow was aware of the sharp glance that Turner shot in Wilson's direction. Wilson ignored it, but Crow guessed its import. There were two local men up at that house, searching, and Turner was thinking that Crow wasn't prepared to delegate to them the sort of responsibility they needed. He was going to check them, poke his nose in. It didn't matter that Turner did not understand. Crow had no intention of disturbing the two officers or calling their competence into question. It was simply that he wanted to check on progress, and more important, he wanted to go into Lendon's house. Into his house, and his life and his personality and his desires and his hates. Only that way would the man emerge, and only in that way, possibly, would his killer appear as a real and not a shadowy figure. Crow placed his bony hands on the table and looked at Wilson.

'But first of all, we three have a call to make.'

It was no more than a ten-minute drive across town and though Wilson and Turner engaged in desultory conversation Crow remained quiet. He was suffering from a certain feeling of guilt; he was aware that he'd hardly thought of Martha during these last few days, although in his usual uxorious fashion he'd phoned her last night. It wasn't simply that he'd not thought of her, though: it was the fact that Mrs Alex Bell was never far from his mind. She was an impressive woman, he decided, with a sigh.

Brian Philips's office was small, cramped and slack as far as business was concerned. The solicitor himself received the three policemen in his room at the top of the stairs and told his single assistant, a shorthand-typist, to turn away any callers for a while. Then he sat down and waved them to chairs. He was wearing a dark brown suit and dark tan shoes, his shirt was cream, his tie green. His mousy hair was smoothed carefully down on his scalp, which glistened through creamily at the temples.

'I have a confession to make, Mr Philips.' Crow's tone lacked affability. 'I asked you to come to Lendon's office yesterday. It was on a pretext. I apologize for that. But it served its purpose.'

'Purpose?' Philips coughed to eradicate a nervous tension that was apparent in his voice. 'I admit to being somewhat surprised to being asked to go there to answer questions about Charles Lendon and the firm but . . . purpose?'

'That's right. I wanted Miss Tennant to hear you speaking in the room-you didn't know, of course, that she was in the anteroom when you quarrelled with Lendon.'

Brian Philips was silent but his eyes were round with disbelief. Crow leaned forward and placed a folder on the desk in front of Philips. He tapped it with a long bony finger.

'There's also the matter of the files.'

'Files?'

'Files. The ones you abstracted from Charles Lendon's office before you hit Constable Pitt over the head.'

'You must be mad! What on earth are you trying to—'

'I see no reason why I shouldn't let you know that protestation is pointless. You knew how to get into that office . . . you'd worked there long enough. You broke into Lendon's room, took the files, assaulted the constable and made your escape. What you didn't realize was that Lendon kept duplicates of the files in the anteroom. This one here contains copies of the papers you took away with you. In one of the red files.'

Philips licked his lips and stared at the folder, trying to read its inscription. Crow made no attempt to make it easy for him by turning the folder around.

'I suppose recovery of this file became necessary after you murdered Lendon,' he said casually.

A grunt escaped explosively from Philips's chest and he sat up with a start. He opened his mouth but no words came: there was only a ludicrous eddying noise from his stomach. Crow nodded.

'It fits, I suppose. You argued with Lendon in his office — he heard a great deal but the closed door fogged your voice and she didn't recognize it again until I asked you in to talk with me. Was it the file you were arguing over? Was his refusal to give it to you the spur that made you kill him?'

'Ridiculous!'

Philips was leaning forward, holding his churning stomach. Crow eyed him narrowly. 'Your statement, taken at the station, is that you were at home, in front of the television set, and fast asleep during the early evening. There is no one to substantiate that. You're a bachelor. No friends were with you. You *could* have been up at the Old Mill!'

'Ridiculous!' Philips gasped again.

'Tell him, Turner, tell him what's in the file here. Tell him, and give him a possible motive for the murder of Charles Lendon.'

Turner hitched his chair forward. Crow's even attack, delivered almost in a monotone, had fascinated him. For a moment he stumbled over his words, then became more fluent.

'The file . . . the red folder . . . well . . . the folder contains papers relevant to three cases dealt with by this firm. The first was before the court in 1968. It concerned a Mrs Delaney who became entitled to a transfer of shares in a private company. Her name should have been entered on the register of members in October, 1965; until this was done, even though she'd paid for the shares, she was not in law a shareholder in the company. In December 1966 she presented a petition for the winding up of the

92

company. The petition was dismissed because the shares had not been properly registered under the Companies Act 1948. She could have sued her legal adviser. She never did.'

'*You* were her legal adviser,' Crow said decisively to Philips.

'The second case,' continued Turner, 'concerned a Mrs Holmes, whose husband died in a car accident. It would seem that because of your negligence her claim for damages failed for want of prosecution. Yet she never sued the firm.'

'Charles Lendon must have possessed considerable influence,' Crow said, 'or perhaps he knew the lady in question?'

'The third case,' Turner went on with heavy emphasis, 'was in 1967. According to this file a limited company was floated in 1963 by three entrepreneurs who issued a prospectus which invited the public to take up shares. There were at least two statements in that prospectus which were patently untrue, but to date no prosecution has been instigated for this offence. There are further details concerning the running of the company which make strange reading. In particular, there is the payment of some £1,000 to a man called Formann. It would seem that he had been guilty of embezzlement — which means, of course, that he could have been dismissed without notice, and a prosecution brought against him. Instead, his service contract was terminated and he was given the sum mentioned by way of compensation for the termination.'

'Perhaps you'd care to comment?' Crow asked pleasantly. When Philips made no reply he waved to Turner to continue.

'This file suggests that the reason why Formann's contract was so terminated was that while he had to be got rid of, he also had to have his silence bought. The fact was, he knew that the company had been indulging in fraudulent trading, and threatened that if he were prosecuted for embezzlement he'd see to it that the whole company came down with him.'

'The company is still in business, it seems,' Crow added. 'No prosecutions brought, no civil proceedings taken against the directors. And again according to this file, one Mr Brian Philips accepts a retainer to act as legal adviser to the company, and the file documents that he had full knowledge of the trading frauds and the false prospectus!'

'I didn't . . . you can't make out that I killed Lendon because of all this!'

Philips was leaning forward in his chair, his elbows on his knees, his hands dangling. He was staring at the floor. 'I didn't kill Lendon, I wanted to, hell, I wanted to!'

'Didn't this constitute motive?'

Philips stared at the file and then swore in a sudden violence of spirit.

'You don't know the sort of man he was! He was always so damned *right,* always so righteous. . .even in spite of the way he ran around after women.'

'But he was efficient in his business dealings.'

'All right, I admit *I* was careless — Mrs Delaney wanted to sue, but Lendon saw her first and persuaded her to settle. Then he made me pay her.'

'What was wrong with that?'

Philips ignored Crow's cold tones. He was launched and hardly heard the inspector.

'Later, in the Holmes fiasco, he settled that again. I think he knew her well but he made me pay her £15,000 and that was far more than was necessary, in my view. It meant I had to sell most of my share in the firm to him to raise the money, and all the time the money my father left me was dwindling. . .'

'Through your negligent handling of business affairs.'

'All right! But Lendon could have *helped* me, instead of being so damned righteous and making me pay up. He could have covered up and—'

'He could hardly cover up the last matter.'

Philips glared at Crow; he seemed to have lost all capacity to think rationally in the matter.

'It wasn't a question of covering up there — he used it to kick me out of the firm. He threw me out, paid me no compensation—'

'I would hardly have thought you were entitled to any. Surely you'd endangered the firm itself?'

'Ah, you don't understand. Lendon hated me! He never let me forget he was the senior partner, never let me forget he brought in the lion's share of the work.'

'Why did you quarrel with him just before he died?'

Philips hesitated, as though wondering whether to admit to it, then he shrugged despondently.

'My firm hasn't been doing too well: since Lendon kicked me out I've had no luck. My managing clerk recently left me during an important case and I . . . well, I needed money. I came to Lendon, asked him, told him that since my father had helped build Lendon, Philips and Barrett I shouldn't have been kicked out without a penny.'

'But you'd agreed to those conditions.'

'Under duress. He could have got me struck off the roll.'

'Instead, he allowed you to continue in practice. I would hardly regard his conduct as reprehensible.'

'Don't bloody moralize to me, Inspector! I . . .' Philips stopped speaking and stared at Crow. After a moment he shook himself like a dog emerging from water. 'You've had me going; I've said things I shouldn't have. You know of my inadequacy as a lawyer, but you can't link me with Lendon's death.'

'Because you've covered your tracks well?'

'Because I didn't kill him.'

Crow leaned back in his chair and stroked his long chin. He nodded slowly.

'Yes, I know you're a poor lawyer. But 'I know also you quarrelled with Lendon and that you're likely now to be charged with offences regarding the third case in this file. It's not for me to say; it's not my affair. But I *am* concerned with Lendon's death, and I think in a matter of hours I'll be able to prove it was you who entered his office last night.'

'There were two other files taken! Why does it have to be me?'

'They were both relatively innocuous. You took them to confuse the trail, but you should have checked them first. Besides, you were the one who'd know the easy route into the office . . . and can you account for your movements last night?'

Brian Philips hesitated, then managed a thin smile.

'I've already disobeyed the precept a lawyer advises his client to observe — say nothing until legal representation is available. It's said that a lawyer makes a bad client. I've nothing more to say, Inspector.'

Crow rose and picked up the file from the desk. He stared at it, resting one bony hand on the desk. At last, wordlessly, he handed the folder to Turner.

'Don't move too far from office or home, Mr Philips.'

As the three policemen drove back to headquarters, Turner ventured a question. 'Will we be charging him, sir?'

'If we can *prove* he was at the office last night, then it'll be breaking and entering, burglary, theft, but murder . . . I don't know . . .'

'His activity may be just tangential,' Wilson said.

'Tangential? That has a ring, Wilson, I like it, I'll adopt it. Tangential activity. It's what you think, isn't it, Wilson? You're convinced there's another direction we should be moving in; an aspect of Lendon's character we haven't looked into. His liking for women. In other words . . .'

'*Cherchez la femme.*'

Crow smiled grimly and nodded in reluctant agreement. 'Admirably put, Wilson, admirably put. And you could quite possibly be right.'

Chapter 11

Cathy found it even more difficult to concentrate on the work in hand, in spite of the fact that the deeper currents of excitement in the office were now subsiding. Words and images continually thronged in her mind, jostling for attention: Charles Lendon, his hand on her shoulder, the muffled tones of Brian Philips through the door of the anteroom, Lendon's hostile expression when he'd seen her with Mike, Carson's angry, puzzled and despairing face.

And the folder in the filing cabinet and the crumpled letter she had taken.

She had half expected Mike to call at her flat last night but he hadn't done so and she'd been thankful for that: now, this evening, she'd have to face another long, lonely time, wondering anxiously about the letter . . .

She finished work at five-thirty and returned to her flat. She drew the curtains across but left the room in darkness. She sat on the settee and put her head back, curling her feet up under her. She closed her eyes but the fears still remained twisting in her mind — the same fears she'd experienced these last few days.

At seven she switched on the light and made herself a sandwich and coffee. Her head was aching. She was carrying the coffee back into the sitting-room when she heard the doorbell ringing. She hesitated and then put down the cup and the plate, walked to the door and opened it. It was Mike. His face was grim, but there was a strained lift to his mouth as he tried to smile.

'Dried already?'

'What?'

'Your hair. You said you were washing it. Every night. Or perhaps you haven't washed it yet. Or perhaps you weren't going to wash it at all. Can I come in or do I stay here in the doorway?'

'No!'

His grin was not a natural one, but he was doing his best to keep his distress under control. She was aware of it, and it weakened her, but frightened her too.

'Now,' he said, 'what precisely does that mean grammatically? That I can't come in or that I can't stay in the doorway? I hope, pray and trust that it's the latter.'

'No. You can't come in,' Cathy said in a rush.

Mike frowned, and the smile faded. His slate-grey eyes grew cold. 'What's the matter? You have someone with you?'

'Yes.'

'You're a liar. I saw you come out of the office. I followed you home. I waited outside. I didn't make a move until your light came on, but I know you've been all alone up here. What the hell's going on, Cathy? What's the matter? You won't see me, you won't speak to me on the phone, you won't come out with me, and now you're behaving in the craziest fashion!'

'Please, Mike—'

'There's no 'please Mike' about it! Either I'm coming in or you're coming out! It might end up with my settling on your doorstep for the night. The landlady might enjoy that.'

'Mike, I'm not well,' Cathy said, almost in tears. 'I just don't feel like going out, and things have been so difficult at the office—'

'I don't see why that should affect our relationship.'

'Mike—'

'Which is it? In, out, or my bawling on your step?'

Cathy took a deep breath, Mike was standing there, broadly, his head thrust forward in a decisive, stubborn attitude and she knew that this was one argument that she wasn't going to win. Perhaps it would be better this way, perhaps she could make a clean break tonight, a break that would snap his affection, wound his pride, force him to leave her alone. She had to hurt him . . . perhaps it was the best way. If she had the resolve to do it. She blinked back her tears.

'Come in for a moment. I'll just clean up a little and get my coat and we'll go out.'

'That's better.' Somewhat mollified, he stumped in behind her. She closed the door carefully. She said no more but left him immediately and went to the bathroom. When she returned he was sitting on the settee, thumbing through a magazine, another one discarded on the floor at his feet. She received the impression that he was seeing little on the printed page. He rose as she entered.

'Ready?'

She nodded. He made no attempt to help her with her coat but remained standing by the door with shoulders hunched until she joined him. Wordlessly they left the house and walked across to his car. The street was as silent as her flat; just one engine, further down the road, coughed into life as she slid into the passenger seat of Mike's car.

He drove silently. He took her down through the town and out to the bypass that circled to the north side of Insterley. They were on the top of the hill, looking across Kenton Wood; and Canthorpe twinkled below them, the jewelled lights of the town centre shining red and green and yellow in the surrounding darkness. She thought for a moment that he was going to pull in at the top of the hill, near one of the firebreaks, but he didn't. He drove on till they reached the Bear Inn and then turned the car to the far end of the rear car park. It was dark there and there were no other vehicles near them. Mike swung towards her.

'Now then, what's it all about?'

She wasn't ready; prevarication was necessary. 'I think I would like a drink.' He glared at her stonily, then thumped open his door.

She got out unaided and followed him into the inn. He demanded two whiskies, in a loud voice, and she took a seat near the fire. There was one other couple in the lounge, and they were on the point of leaving. By the time Mike brought the two glasses across they had gone.

Some of the whisky spilled as he placed the glasses carelessly on the table.

'I'll repeat the question. What the hell is it all about? What's got into you? Why are you avoiding me?'

Cathy sipped at the whisky. He'd been right in getting her this. . .she was going to need it, to hold her nerve. When she looked up at him her eyes were calm.

'You're right, Mike. I have been avoiding you.'

'Why?'

'It's quite simple. Can't you guess?'

He looked at her and laughed in disbelief, but there was no humour in the sound. 'Don't be so bloody puerile! You trying to tell me you've met someone else?'

'That sounds either uncomplimentary to me, or egotistical of you, but yes, I have met someone else.'

'And decided that I'm not the great love in your life? In just a couple of days? Credit me with some sense, Cathy, for God's sake!'

'Sense or not, it's the truth.'

Her tone was reserved, and her eyes were steady. For one brief moment she thought that he almost believed her and then the angry light in his eyes died, and something warmer, more protective took its place. Her heart sank.

'I can't accept that, Cathy. I know you, better than you think. I know you don't give your love lightly, and that when you do give it there's a permanency about it that would prevent the sort of attitude that you're now trying to tell me you've adopted. It's something else. Something's happened to upset you, and for some reason you're taking it out on me.'

'Nothing has happened.'

'I know different. You're anxious, and you're worried and . . . yes, you're scared too, about something. What's it all about, Cathy?'

'I—'

Perhaps it was the earnest tone in his voice, or the pleading, loving look in his eyes, but in that moment she almost told him. But she remembered the words in the letter, and she remembered Lendon, and she thought that in spite of everything . . . she couldn't speak, it was better to break with Mike, they could never exist together with this shadow between them, and she clutched at her whisky glass in desperation and downed the drink.

'Cathy!'

Mike caught at her arm. His lips were compressed and deep in his grey eyes there was a flickering hardness that she hadn't seen before. It was a watchfulness, an animal wariness that touched her skin coldly. She felt his fingers digging into the flesh of her upper arm.

'Cathy, what's happened? Something at the office, that's it, isn't it? Something has happened at the office!'

'Nothing has happened. Nothing. This. . .this has just been a mistake, that's all. I want to break it off. I don't want to see you again. I'm no longer certain about my feelings for you, and I don't want to go on. Let's just leave it at that. Let's part friends, and leave it at that, Mike. Please.'

'The office,' he muttered, almost to himself. The eyes flickered at her, calculating. She stood up.

'This was a mistake. I want to go home, Mike.' He rose, to stand glaring at her.

'Lendon,' he said thickly. 'That bloody Lendon. What have you found out, Cathy?'

'Nothing. It's as I said, damn you! I just want to finish it. Why do men have to be so blasted vain? I tell you I just don't love you anymore, and I want to go home!'

'Of course!' There was a naked viciousness in his voice now. 'Lendon. Now he's dead, the police will have been going through everything. And in that office you'll have seen his files. You'll have read all about it!'

Her heart was beating at a terrifying pace, and she swung away from him to walk towards the door. He called her name, caught her at the door, held it closed against her to prevent her leaving.

'All right, so now you've read Lendon's files! I can't see that it should affect us, Cathy! What's it got to do with us? Why must it affect us in this way?'

She pushed him aside, dragged the door open from his restraining hand, and ran out into the car park.

'I don't understand you!' he shouted.

She walked quickly past his car and he ran after her, grabbing at her arm, again. His face was blank, featureless in the darkness. He was a stranger.

'For God's sake, Cathy, we can't leave it like this! Why on earth should my quarrel with Lendon break us up in this way?'

She tore herself away from his fierce grip and half ran out of the car park to the road. There were three cars stationed in the front park and one across the other side of the road, on the grass verging on Kenton Wood, but there seemed to be no one around to hear Mike shout again.

'I suppose you're going to damn well walk home, now! Cathy! What the hell's got into you?'

She ran on. Tears began to trickle down her cheeks, but she ran on and crossed the road, scrambling through the long grass at the verge and into the firebreak leading down through the woods. It would take her over the hill dipping down to where the road that ran into Canthorpe lay, about three-quarters of a mile below. She could get a bus there, for it was early, nearer eight than nine. Mike called her name again, just once, but she ran on. She went down over the first slope and the lights of the inn vanished, and then there was only the darkness and the silence of the trees to take the harsh rasping of her breath.

At the foot of the short slope Cathy stopped, standing in the darkness of the firebreak, and the sobbing started, part harsh breathing, part crying. She let it go on for almost a minute, before she was able to tell herself to stop, pull herself together.

'*Cathy!*'

Mike's voice, from the top of the hill. Cathy shook her head, and began to walk on again determinedly. It was better this way. If she stayed with him, if he comforted her, caressed her, she would collapse, her resolve would break, she'd tell him she'd found the letter and he would discover that she knew everything. And then it would be impossible . . . everything would be impossible. He would have a decision to make, and she would be burdening him with that decision.

It was better that she left him now, cut free. He need never know that she had guessed what happened the night Charles Lendon died. He need never tell her why it happened, or how. This way was better. She could walk on, and leave him and . . . Cathy slowed, then stopped. It wasn't the firebreak. Ahead of her was the blank wall of trees, solid and thick, barring her progress. She wasn't on the firebreak at all; it was simply an entry which now ran, narrowing, round to the left. She realized too that the ground was rutted with tractor marks. This track was used for dragging out logs after thinning. She glanced back up the slope, to the hazy skyline, then looked down ahead of her again.

If she followed this track to the left it would almost inevitably come to a logging clearing, and then a firebreak which she could take down the hill. It made little difference. She couldn't get lost. It was just a matter of going down the hill, and then she would inevitably reach the main road. It was just a bit longer this way, that was all. She strode out confidently.

She followed the track to the left and it was just the width of a tractor and a few feet more. The night was dark. There was no moon, and the trees were tall, peaked against pale, cloud-drifted stars. Her breath stained the darkness whitely, and the cold breeze running up the hill came soughing through the lifting branches. She moved quietly down the pathway, stumbling occasionally, conscious of the cold darkness, but there was no reason why she should feel frightened. Yet the scuttling sound in the undergrowth to her right, as a small furry body thrust its way through the bushes, brought a sudden fear leaping to her throat and she stood stock still, listening. The scuttling noise faded and died. And she was suddenly aware that Mike had followed her.

It was a curious feeling. She knew Mike. She loved him. But he was now scrambling down the track behind her, and the knowledge razored against her nerves. All at once she could think only of the letter in the folder, not of Mike's warm mouth; she could remember only the malice in his face as he spoke of Lendon, not the caressing touch of his hands; she could recall only the new hardness she had seen tonight in his eyes, the quick nervousness of the trapped animal, and the memory of his tenderness was banished.

He was following her down the track, but it was a different Mike from the man she had known, or thought she knew. He was the man who had hated Lendon, he was the man who knew she had seen Lendon's files, he was the man who-

She couldn't bring herself to say it, even to herself. But the scrambling noise on the track around the bend made her heart jump.

Mike was following her. And he was no longer calling her name.

If she made her way along this pathway she would reach a clearing, she would reach the firebreak, she would get down to the main road. But how far ahead was the firebreak? It would be quicker, surely, to go straight through the woods.

Quicker. And perhaps better. Mike would walk on, stick to the track, assume she was ahead.

She struck off to the right, down the hill. The direct route, a half-mile to the main road. It was the best way. But she realized after a moment it was also the noisiest. The bushes crashed under her feet and there was the crackling of breaking twigs, loud in the darkness. Cathy stopped, and stood still. She listened, and her heart thundered.

She was some fifteen yards in from the track that she had been following, and she strained eyes and ears to fix Mike's presence, but there was only the darkness. Mike had stopped moving too . . . he was back on the track somewhere, not far behind her, but like her he must have stopped, to listen. As the implication of his conduct came to her, the quickness of her pulse matched her fear. Mike wasn't following her openly, he wasn't coming after her quickly, calling her name as he had done on the road. He had called her name just once at the end . . . had it been for the benefit of people leaving the inn? But thereafter he had come down the road quietly, stealthily.

Stealth. It was an ugly word. A twig cracked like a pistol shot in the silence, and Cathy turned quickly, plunging more deeply into the woods, hastening down the slope towards the road below. And as she forced her way through the trees she was suddenly aware of a background, almost an echo to the noise of her own progress: the sound of another person forcing his way roughly through the trees.

Her lips moved soundlessly as she ran . . . *crazy, crazy, crazy!* This was Mike she was running from, Mike, the man she wanted to marry! He had come down to make her see sense, return with him to the car, allow him to drive her home sensibly, carefully, quietly, lovingly. But she was running, and his eyes would be angry as he ran after her, cold and hard and angry at the fuss she was making. Over nothing. Was it nothing? He knew she had seen Lendon's files — he knew that — something caught at her breath, and she gasped. Tears began to course down her face and her body was trembling. Trees loomed up waving dark arms at her and she struggled on. She had given up all thought of concealment now as she plunged straight down the slope, and each crashing footstep beat out the words to her — Mike, Mike, Mike!

Mike also had given up all attempt at stealth. She could hear him blundering after her, tearing his way through the trees. She looked back twice but saw nothing in the darkness except the tall pines, but Mike's presence filled the darkness and it was an angry presence, a malignant presence, so that it was terror that now caught at Cathy's throat, unreasoning, as she scrambled down a bank and ploughed her way through soggy dead leaves.

For a quick moment she stopped. She glanced around her, and her native wit overrode her fear. She was in a gully; the bank behind her was matched by another bank in front. She ran a few yards down the gully and her progress was swift, and almost silent. The squelching of the wet leaves was as nothing to the noisy crashing in the woods behind her. She paddled on for another twenty yards or so and then turned, clambered up the bank. Quietly, carefully, she eased her way in among the trees again and the stars were shut out once more. She braced herself, leant against a tree some little distance in and waited. She stood there, absolutely still, her cold hands cupped against her face, her elbows squeezed against her breasts, quelling the pounding of her heart.

The crashing behind her slowed. Suddenly, it stopped.

Mike had reached the top of the bank. Silence flowed in through the wood. Far below her there came the drone of a lorry, winding along the main road and coughing against the hill. A distant dog barked, a light sound, lifted on the night air, sharp, yet tenuous and drifting.

A dark shadow leapt up before her eyes.

He had crossed the ditch; he was standing on the bank, black, formless, listening in a half-crouched position. For one agonized moment she almost called his name, eager for the comforting warmth of his arms, but the crouching menace of his stance choked off her words and she clapped her hands over her mouth, shielded the silvering of her breath against the air. Her lips moved under her cold fingers, framing Mike's name, but the man who stood there, urgent, listening, was a Mike she had never known, a new Mike . . . but a Mike that Charles Lendon must have known. Cathy's knees trembled, and she almost sank to the ground.

Then the shadow was gone. She heard a splash, and realized that Mike had guessed what she hoped he would guess, that she had taken the quiet route, down through the sodden leaves. She heard a crunching sound as he stepped on a frozen patch at the edge of the ditch, and then there was only the silence again.

She waited for perhaps two minutes in that freezing silence and then with consummate care she moved deeper under the trees, and down the slope. There was no sound behind her; perhaps Mike was now out of earshot. With the thought her pace began to quicken and she moved more smoothly. She was among a patch of conifer and the pine needles under her feet were soft and gentle, and the way was clearer with no bushes to bar her way. But the darkness was intense and she moved with hands outstretched before her, almost feeling her way among the trees.

It was almost five minutes before she realized that Mike was behind her again. Once more she stood still and listened, her hand fluttering nervously to her mouth, and she heard him blundering into a tree, and cursing. For a panic-stricken moment she thought she would dodge him again, hide among the dark trees, stay behind as he struggled past, but at the terrifying thought of such a cat and mouse pursuit her nerve broke and she took to flight. She moved hastily through the pines and felt the slope dipping sharply beneath her feet. She heard a car below, and it was not far away. The road must be near; few yards farther and she caught the flash of headlights. But the faint illumination did something else: it outlined her, moving among the straight pines, and she heard a subdued grunt. Mike had seen her.

Cathy threw caution to the wind. She plunged forward, scraped her knee against a tree, and then she was out of the pines and the going was rougher as dead frozen fern and wild rose-bushes dragged at her legs, and the scrub alder and larch tore at her clothes. She heard Mike's heavy body thrusting through the bushes behind her, not fifty yards away, and she ran on, gasping feverishly, a pain rising in her chest, her heart thumping against her ribs. *Mike! Mike! Mike!*

When the branch caught at her arm she almost fainted. It dragged her to a stop abruptly, and she found difficulty in retaining her balance. The twigs were entwined in her dress and coat; she pulled frantically at them and they crackled frostily and broke but she was still held and behind her there was the crashing of Mike's progress, the rasping of his angry breath. The sounds of his pursuit were suddenly animal, and unfocused. She lost their direction. They seemed almost to come from two directions behind her as though his anger had spread out like wings in the

108

forest to engulf her. She tore at the restraining branch, glanced back to see the dark form rise up fifteen yards away and screamed, dragging despairingly at the branch as it gave way.

Then Cathy was running down the slope on to a narrow pathway, and the starlight was above her and she was bursting out into the short-grassed clearing at the verge of the woods. The crashing behind her increased, whirling in its savage, disappointed violence, but she was away from the grass verge. In her ears there was the ringing of tarmac, hard and black under her feet, but almost at once it was blotted out by the harsh, high screeching of brakes and the headlights leapt at her like a wild-eyed tiger.

Chapter 12

After the two constables had packed Lendon's loose papers in the car, Mrs Bell asked Crow if he'd like a cup of coffee before he left. He did not ask himself why he accepted: it was not something he would normally have done, accepting such an offer in such a situation, but he could have said that his acceptance was motivated by a desire to get more about Lendon's background from her, and more about her relationship with Lendon. Nevertheless, had he asked the question of himself he would have been forced to admit that it was the sheer pleasure of watching her and hearing her low, modulated voice that played an important part in his acceptance.

They sat downstairs in Lendon's sitting-room. Crow had looked briefly over her flat and there seemed little point in going up to its cramped confinement when there was room downstairs like this. Mrs Bell sipped at the strong coffee and glanced up at Crow; her eyes were dark, and direct.

'Did they find anything that might be of assistance?'

'The two constables? Well, I don't know yet. There's a lot of stuff there, and a large number of what appear to be legal papers. We'll be down at the station tomorrow sorting them out. We'll see then.'

'And you have no leads yet as to who might have . . . murdered Charles?'

He smiled faintly, and made no attempt to answer. His patent reluctance brought a brief smile to her own face. He was pleased at her sensitivity, and quick reaction. 'You must forgive me,' she said, 'but women are constitutionally inquisitive.'

'It's part of their charm,' Crow replied gallantly. 'Is your brother calling tonight?'

Alex Bell shook her head; Crow had been right about the russet hue, for he caught the light behind her hair now and his guess was confirmed.

'No, John is staying at the hostel in Canthorpe, as usual. He'll probably be out to see me tomorrow afternoon: he often does come then.'

Crow weighed his words carefully.

'You said, last time we met, that your brother had not had a happy life. He seems very much on edge to me; has he any record of nervous trouble over a long period?'

The woman sitting across the room from him nodded, her handsome features smooth and calm.

'I'm afraid he has. You see, John was the third child. My elder brother, Henry, was killed in the war at about the same time as . . . as my husband. John was the youngest and was very much protected by Mother, so that when she died my brother Henry looked after him. When Henry was killed John turned to me. But . . . well, Mother had always spoiled him, you know . . . I think she wanted him to be dependent upon her. And I suppose I'm no better than Mother. I was eighteen when my husband died, and John came to me and I was able to help him through school with the insurance money. But I organized John's life, made him dependent on *me*. I was selfish-you know? I used John to assuage my own grief.'

'Your conduct hardly seems selfish to me.'

'John did quite well at school. He got a job in a bank later and was happy for a while, but I think things got on top of him somewhat. There was a girl . . . well, I never felt much could come of it, she wasn't good enough for him, and certainly when he found out she'd been sleeping with some other man when she was supposed to be engaged to John . . .' Mrs Bell shrugged. 'It broke him up, and there was little I could do other than offer sympathy. He's had various jobs, but it's a bit difficult since he attends Linwood, and lives in for periods of time. There's nothing *wrong* with him, you must understand, he just gets depressed, I think he remembers . . .'

'He comes to see you regularly. That must help.'

'Yes. He has that old car . . . I help him financially, of course.'

Poor John Barnes: mother-ridden, sister-fixated, and on the receiving end of an unhappy love affair. Crow should have felt stirrings of sympathy but there were none. He didn't like Barnes though he couldn't tell why.

Mrs Bell leaned forward. 'May I ask you something?'

Crow didn't like the sound of that but he nodded and smiled.

'As long as it's not too personal, and doesn't involve my breaking the Official Secrets Act.' She returned his smile, but warily.

'It is personal, in a sense. I want to ask you . . . I told you that I became Charles Lendon's mistress quite deliberately, in an attempt to secure my future; when I told you that, what was your reaction? I mean, you took it very calmly, but what did you *think*?'

'I'm a policeman, Mrs Bell—'

'You're also a man. I want you to tell me: was I wrong in behaving like that seven years ago? Do you think I was wrong?'

Crow struggled for an appropriate answer.

'I . . . I don't know. You must realize that I'm not here to pass judgments. You did what you thought fit at the time; I don't think anyone can castigate you socially for that. It was your life. You were hurting no one, except perhaps yourself.'

'Charles was a very attractive man, and I thought that in time he would marry me . . . but it's no matter. The house will be mine now, and all ends well, I suppose. It's just that I only wish that he had . . .'

She looked at him levelly. There was a hint of self-mockery in her dark eyes. 'You know, he never once told me that he loved me.'

Crow was getting out of his depth. He finished his coffee and stumbled to his feet, suddenly more conscious than ever of his skeletal height, and his awkwardness, and his gaunt, unlovely appearance. Mrs Bell rose with him and he looked down at her. In a way he could understand why she asked such questions of him, a stranger. He could understand her need to confide in someone, to talk about herself and Charles Lendon, and John Barnes too, for that matter. She was a handsome woman, and a proud one, he had no doubt. She would not have spoken like this to anyone she knew. A stranger was different. He felt a little sorry for her. And yet he knew it could be misplaced. Softly, he said:

'Such inhibitions wouldn't have been Charles Lendon's alone. It's my wife's constant complaint that I don't tell her these days.'

Alex Bell smiled at him.

'At least that implies you did once upon a time.'

And, he mused, as he took his leave of Mrs Bell, he supposed he *did* use to tell Martha, once. In his youth. Why was it that people might feel love deepen, become warmer, but in the greater security of passing time become less demonstrative of that love? A paradox.

But what the hell had John Crow been doing talking about love with Alex Bell, anyway? He had a murder case on his hands and there he was sitting drinking coffee with a handsome widow and discussing mistresses and motivations and love. It was time he got back on the rails.

Nevertheless, his mind kept drifting back to Mrs Bell as he drove through the darkness along the road to town, drifting back to the pleasant sight she presented sitting stiff-backed and upright in her chair, her russet-dark hair swept back, her slim hands in her lap, those magnificent eyes holding his . . .

It was partly because his mind was still on Alexandra Bell that John Crow almost failed to take evasive action when the girl ran out into the road in front of him.

She leapt out, her face white against the headlights and he wrenched the wheel sideways. The car bucked and the brakes screeched as he thumped both feet down, then he was swinging across the road, skidding, and his headlights flashed across and round in a wide arc, road, trees, road, trees . . .

He was stalled, facing the way he had come. The night was quiet, except for the clicking of the girl's shoes on the road and then sobbing breath, harsh outside the car door. His black, angry excitement vanished when he saw who it was.

'Miss Tennant! What on earth-!'

Crow opened the door quickly and got out; the girl was holding her throat with one hand, and leaning against the car with the other. She was gasping for breath.

'What's the matter?' he asked quickly, taking her arm. 'Here, get in the car!'

She shook her head but allowed him to draw her into the car, where she slumped down in the seat.

'It's all right, Inspector. It's just that I came running down the bank . . . and then your headlights . . . I thought you were going to knock me down, and . . . it drove all the breath out of me. I'm all right, really I am. Just shocked, that's all.'

Crow eyed the girl carefully. In the interior light of the car he could see her dishevelled condition, the paleness of her cheek, the broken bits of twig on her coat. Instinctively, he looked back towards the woods stretching above, dark and menacing against the skyline. The girl touched his arm.

'I *am* all right, really.'

It was as though she was unwilling for his thoughts to turn towards the trees.

'If you don't mind my saying so, you look considerably distressed. Are you sure nothing's wrong?'

She managed an embarrassed laugh and attempted to smooth down her skirt and extract some of the twigs from her hair.

'The fact is, Inspector, I . . . I was walking across the top there and came down through the woods, and got a bit lost, then a bit frightened, you know how it is in the darkness when you can't see a thing. I got a bit tangled in the bushes. Then, when I saw the road I was so pleased I was out that I ran down, and the slope was steeper than I thought and there I was, right in the path of your car.'

There was an odd pleading in her tone. She wanted desperately to be believed, and yet Crow had heard nothing less convincing in his life. She was a poor liar and he had come across some of the best. She had had a reason for entering those trees and something had frightened her in the woods, right enough, but it hadn't been just the darkness. She didn't want to talk about it. In Crow's book that could only mean that the person who had frightened her was known to her, and she didn't want to involve him in trouble. As Crow stared at her impassively the thought came to him that this matter might not be unconnected with the piece of information that he was convinced she was withholding from him. She would bring it out in time, if he were patient, but that didn't mean that he should simply remain completely passive in the matter. Abruptly he slid his long body behind the driving wheel.

'Well, if you're sure you're all right, Miss Tennant, the least I can do is drive you home, even if you did almost wreck the car and put me through the windscreen in the process.'

'Inspector, I'm terribly sorry. Truly.'

She was, but he also detected in her tone a tremor of relief because he seemed to have accepted her story. As he started the engine and turned the car in the road, his headlights briefly flashed over the trees again. For a moment he thought he caught a brief, answering flash, as though someone had flicked a torch through the trees, but as the car moved up the hill, and his eyes glanced along the outlined pines and thick undergrowth of bushes, he dismissed the thought as imagination. Nevertheless, he wondered what else, or who else could be in there among the pines.

The journey back to town and to her flat was silent.

He made no attempt to ask how she had got there in the first instance, who had driven her, why she was walking. He was busy with other considerations. When he dropped her off at the flat he waited until she had gone inside. As she was doing so a car's headlights briefly turned into the road. The car stopped, reversed, and went on its way. Crow looked after it thoughtfully. It could have been someone taking a wrong turning. On the other hand . . .

When he got back to the Warwick Arms, where he and Wilson had rooms, he went straight upstairs for a quick wash, and then came down to the lounge bar. Wilson was already sitting there, with an evening paper and a glass of beer. He caught sight of Crow, and called to the barman for another half of bitter. Crow sat down beside Wilson, who folded away his newspaper, and the two sipped silently at their beer for a moment.

'Developments?' Crow asked.

Wilson shrugged, and twisted his broad face into an unhelpful grimace.

'I've been through the Charlton file but there's not much there. As far as I can see, Charles Lendon employed this enquiry agent, Charlton, for a client who lives in London. Hampstead. A chap called Kent — a dentist, I understand. There's nothing in the file to say precisely what he was looking for, though I gather it has something to do with Kent's wife.'

'Divorce proceedings?'

'Looks like. But there's not a single thing in the file about Charlton's final report to Lendon. On the other hand, there is a letter from Lendon to Kent to the effect that he has been unable to discover anything to suggest that Mrs Kent had been conducting an affair with anyone in Canthorpe.'

'Hmm. I think it would be wise to have a word with Mr Kent as soon as possible. Probably a dead end, but I'd really like to know who, if anyone, Mr Kent was suspicious of.'

'Well, it wouldn't be Lendon, sir, would it? Kent wouldn't employ him to conduct an enquiry if he was the one who was cuckolding him.'

'We'll follow it up, anyway, Wilson. See what we find. Two other matters also. Lendon's papers from his house: they've been taken to the station tonight so we'll have to go through them tomorrow. I think you'd better supervise that and let Turner go chasing Mr Kent. The other matter concerns Miss Tennant.'

Briefly he told Wilson what had happened on his way back from the Lendon house. There were certain inspectors, he knew, who preferred to keep some lines of investigation to themselves, in the mistaken assumption that to tell another of their suspicions inevitably meant a destruction of secrecy and a confession of weakness. Crow believed in keeping Wilson entirely in the picture.

'What I want to know, Wilson, is just who she was with this evening. To start with, I imagine she has a boy-friend?'

'Well, I understood from one of the assistant solicitors — Parnell, I think — that she's been going out with a young man for the last two months or so.'

Crow pursed his fleshy lips.

'I don't know what conclusions you've reached about Miss Tennant, but I'm sure she knows more than she tells us. I'm convinced that she has information which it worries her to keep back from us. Now tonight, she was equally anxious that I should believe her nonsensical story about going out for a walk, getting worried in the dark, and running out to the main road. I want to know whom she is protecting, and what information she has. So as a first step we must get her background, and find out about her social life.'

He took a long draught of beer and caught the barman's eye to order another for Wilson and one for himself.

'As for me,' he said, 'I think I'll have a session tomorrow with our respected chief superintendent.'

* * *

Wilson was already at breakfast when Crow came down next morning. It was a fine, crisp day with a watery winter sun hanging low in the morning sky and they decided to walk to the station together. Crow rather liked Canthorpe; true, its centre was a mess of snarling traffic, particularly at this time of the morning, but most towns were like that these days and there were some small, rather interesting-looking alleys running off from the main street, while the poultry cross in the High Street was rather fine, even if it was dwarfed by a garish department store towering high. Crow shuddered as he passed it and Wilson smiled a grim smile: he was used to his inspector's aesthetic quivers.

When they arrived at Canthorpe Police Headquarters Wilson went at once to join the two officers dealing with the material culled from Lendon's house, while Crow had a quick word with Turner, who told him:

'All the thirty files from the office have now been brought here, sir: I've gone through most of them, and written up a précis of contents.'

'Fine. Look, I was going to ask you to see a Mr Kent at Hampstead, but on second thoughts I think we'll ask the local police up there to do the job for us. I want to know why Kent instructed Lendon to look into his wife's movements, what he suspected about his wife and whether he was satisfied about the results. Will you ask one of the CID men to get that sorted out? Then, you get those files finished and as soon as the summary is completed I want to see it. Anything interesting, and I mean particularly interesting, I'll want my attention drawn to. Right?'

Turner nodded and moved away. Crow liked him; a little green, but eager. He'd do. With a sigh Crow moved across to the desk sergeant.

'Chief Superintendent Simpson in yet?'

The desk sergeant looked surprised. From the look he received Crow gathered that the chief superintendent was always in early.

'About twenty minutes ago, sir. But he did have someone with him. Mr Carson.'

'Oh? He still there?'

'I'll check, sir, but he might have gone.'

The sergeant rang through to Simpson's office, spoke briefly and then looked up to Crow.

'Yes, sir, Mr Carson has gone. The super is available if you wish to see him.'

Crow tapped lightly at the door and when he received the grunted reply entered the room.

The craggy head of the chief superintendent was bent over a file on the desk, but he didn't keep Crow waiting. It was a good sign. Simpson was obviously not in one of his surlier moods, even though his mottled face seemed to suggest that his interview with Carson had hardly been amicable.

'Good morning, Crow. How are things going?'

'Well enough, sir, but it's early days, of course.'

'Ahuh. What can I do for you?'

'I've come to ask for your assistance, Chief Superintendent.'

Hugh Simpson's heavy head was still. His eyes narrowed slightly as he stared at Crow and he opened his mouth as though to say something, then closed it again. Crow gained the impression that Simpson was on the point of telling the inspector that he had no intention of meddling, but changed his mind because of the fact that assistance was being openly asked for. It flattered the man's ego. After a moment he relaxed and settled massively back in his chair with a certain air of quiet satisfaction. Crow made no attempt to deny him his triumph.

'I'll do anything I can,' said Simpson pontifically, stroking a hammer of a fist against his dark-bristled chin. 'Sit down for a moment, Inspector.'

Crow sat down and contemplated his long, bony legs. 'There are a couple of things you can help me on . . . you've considerable knowledge of the town and the people, and I haven't.'

'You'd like to know what I can tell you about Charles Lendon, for instance.'

'That'll do for a start.'

'Lendon was a sound businessman, stood no nonsense, and was pretty straight in his dealings. Too straight for some; you know, people don't like to feel in the wrong all the time and there was that chance if you dealt with Lendon. His one big weakness was women, but of recent years he went about things more quietly, I gather.'

'Any current girl-friend?'

'Ah, well . . . heard of a feller called Charlton?'

'Indeed. An enquiry agent who died recently.'

'Don't waste time checking his death. I already have. When one of those bloody irregulars dies on my patch I want to *know*. The thing is, Lendon hired him.'

'For someone called Kent, I gather.'

'That's right. You might find Lendon's girl-friend was Kent's wife.'

Crow thought quietly for a moment.

'Would Kent have engaged a solicitor who was having an affair with his wife?'

'It's a matter of timing. Maybe Lendon looked into her background for the husband and then got interested in her himself. Charlton had certainly been checking on Mrs Kent to back divorce proceedings. Charlton's files, which I've seen, make it clear that Mrs Kent has been involved with a professional gentleman in Canthorpe. I presume he gave that information to Lendon, but Mr Kent never acted upon it.'

'Because Lendon never gave it to him.'

'Is that so?'

'Lendon's file on Kent simply contains a letter to Kent informing him that enquiries by Charlton had been fruitless.'

Simpson leaned forward and grimaced.

'Lendon suppressed the information, eh? So much for my straight businessman!'

'You did say he had a weakness for women,' Crow said quietly. 'Anyway, I'd like to have any further details on the Charlton involvement, please.'

'I'll let you have all the papers.' Simpson laid a hard, horny hand on the desk. 'Anything else?'

'There's a Miss Tennant—'

Simpson extracted a file from his desk. 'I got a breakdown on everyone in that office within three hours of finding Lendon's corpse at the Old Mill. Now then . . . here we are. Catherine Tennant: twenty years old, mother dead, father lives in Stanely, she came to Lendon as an articled clerk nearly three years ago, takes her finals next summer. Stepping out with . . . ah yes, interesting . . . with Michael Enson. Now then, Crow, the name Enson rings a bell. I'm pretty sure there was bad blood between Enson and Lendon . . .'

Simpson rose and paced slowly across the room, his big hands locked behind his back. 'I think it involved Enson's father . . . I'll get one of the constables to check the records.'

'Thank you.'

'Mmm. And that chap Carson — you'll have a crack at him, of course. Damned nuisance. He was around here again this morning telling me I ought to watch the woods, telling me my business! I sent him packing I can tell you, and—'

The telephone cut across his outburst. A brief conversation and he turned to Crow.

'The chief constable wants me. Stay here in the building. I'll only be ten minutes or so. See you shortly.'

Simpson led the way out of the office. Crow could see that the chief superintendent was in good spirits: being asked for advice and assistance by Crow had uplifted him. It obviously made him feel more secure, made him feel that his stand in the first instance had been justified, and perhaps even convinced him that he could have done the job better than the man from the murder squad anyway. Crow smiled quietly to himself. He didn't mind Simpson's euphoria: as long as it brought results, and made easier the working relationship in which they found themselves, that was all that mattered. But Carson's visit this morning; he must try to find out from Simpson what it was about. Obviously it would be connected with Jenny Carson's death, but Carson was also hovering on the fringe of the Lendon enquiry, and it would be as well to keep all ends neatly tied.

Crow walked into the room where Wilson and two other officers were still sifting through the material obtained from Lendon's house.

'The lads are looking at the general stuff,' Wilson explained, 'and I've got what appear to be Lendon's personal papers here. I'll give you a whistle, sir, as soon as I find anything.'

Crow checked his watch. Simpson should be out in ten minutes or so. He walked back towards the desk sergeant. The sergeant raised his head as Crow approached and there was a wary look in his eye. Perhaps it was a look he reserved for all CID men, or perhaps just for outsiders.

'Have you got a map of the Kenton Wood area, in detail?'

The sergeant looked doubtful, but a fresh-faced young constable sitting over a report and a typewriter looked up and said:

'Jenkins drew a special one for the super a week ago, Sarge.'

'Where can I get a look at it?'

'I think it's in the super's office, but if you ask Jenkins he'll tell you, sir. That's him over there, in front of the interview room.'

Jenkins was sure it would be all right for Crow's purposes and led the way into Simpson's room.

'It's over here, sir.'

Jenkins walked across to the table in the corner of the room and pulled open a drawer. He extracted a folded sheet of drawing paper and spread it out on the table. It was an ink drawing traced from an ordnance survey map, with various points marked on it. Crow put his finger on one of the points.

'What's this?'

'That marks the spot where little Jenny Carson's body was found, sir.'

'I see. And this is the Old Mill, up here, where Lendon was murdered . . . What's this building here?'

'That's the Bear Inn, sir, and this area here is Kenton Wood. You can see that it runs along the side of the hill here for almost three miles, but is about three-quarters of a mile wide, and takes in, at its edge, Mr Lendon's property.'

Crow nodded. His mind was shifting to James Carson. 'Tell me, Jenkins, what exactly was all this fuss about the right of way through Woodrow Lane? You know, the cause of the trouble between Lendon and Carson?'

The burly young constable shrugged.

'Well, sir, it was like this. If you take a look at this map you'll see that there's a big council estate south of Lendon's house. Now there's a bus service that runs through the estate, but sometimes kids who have missed the bus, or want to save the bus money they've been given so that they can buy sweets with it, will walk to school. The school lies here, north of Lendon's property, and across the main road.'

'I see. And if children miss the bus they could take the shortest distance to the main road, along Woodrow Lane.'

'That's what they used to do, sir, but there was a bit of vandalism in the lane and Mr Lendon closed it to them. There was a heck of a rumpus about it, but Mr Lendon insisted that he was within his rights, and it seemed that he was. There was no legal right of way through Woodrow Lane.'

'So what happened then?'

'Simply that kids missing the bus would have to go the long way round through the estate — or they could take a short cut, even shorter than the Woodrow Lane one, through the Kenton Wood to the main road.'

'And that's what Jenny Carson did.'

'Seems like, sir. The morning was dark. She didn't take the bus, she walked through the wood and someone murdered her. We didn't find the body until early next morning. You'll see that she was dragged some distance from what would be the natural way through the wood.'

Crow grimaced. He had an unpleasant feeling at the pit of his stomach at the thought of that poor terrified child in the half-morning light, and he remembered James Carson's veiled, pain-ridden eyes when he had spoken to him at the Carson house.

'You'll have checked all known sex-offenders in the locality, of course.'

'Yes, sir. Within twenty-four hours of finding the body we'd checked them all. Ever since, we've been taking statements . . . you know, we must have hundreds, thousands of the damn things to go through here in the station. You know the drill, sir, checking for discrepancies and all that. But it'll take months—'

'And while it continues Woodrow Lane has remained closed, and pressure was still being brought upon Charles Lendon,' mused Crow. 'But you still haven't produced any positive leads on the Carson child killing, and children are still running the risk of sexual assault and murder in the woods.'

He was not really talking to Jenkins at all; his words were spoken in a low tone, almost to himself, for his mind was drifting on his own problems, seeking the half-sighted truths, and he was not consciously concerning himself with the Jenny Carson murder. But preoccupied as he was, he could not fail to notice the cold silence which fell upon the room after his remarks. He looked up from the map at Jenkins, and the young constable's face was white. Even as Crow turned to look in the direction in which Jenkins was staring, Simpson's voice cut harshly across the room.

'All right, Jenkins, that will do!'

The constable stumbled out as quickly as he could. A little puzzled, Crow stared at the chief superintendent, standing just inside the door of the room with the chief constable chubbily unhappy behind him. Simpson's previous good humour had evaporated; his brow was now thunderous and his jaw granite-hard. Crow opened his mouth to speak, but Simpson beat him to it.

125

'What the hell do you think you're up to?'

Crow's immediate reaction was surprise but it was short-lived; his heart sank as he thought of the low tones in which he had spoken those last words to Jenkins. Reflective they had been, conspiratorial they had not, but to Simpson, entering the room and finding Crow and the constable poring over the map prepared in connection with the Carson murder, the inference would not be an unreasonable one to make.

'I think I should explain—' began Crow, but Simpson interrupted him furiously, stalking forward into the room. His face was ugly with anger, and his fists were balled.

'You're damned right you'd better explain! What the hell do you think you're doing? You're in my room, going over a map prepared for me, concerned with the Carson investigation, and you're discussing the conduct of that investigation with a junior officer!'

'I was not doing that,' Crow said defensively. 'At least, I know that was what it looked like, but in fact the only reason I wanted to see the map was because I wanted some idea of the argument that had developed between Lendon and Carson and—'

'Then why the hell were you discussing my investigation?' Simpson was beside himself in his fury. 'Let's get one thing straight, Crow! You came in here this morning and asked for my assistance. All right. I gave it freely. If you want to know, it even gave me pleasure to give you information: it just proved to me that I was right and I could have handled the whole damn thing myself in the first instance!'

'Hugh—' The chief constable attempted to break in, but Simpson was launched and would not be restrained.

'The fact that I was prepared to give you information and assistance, and the fact that I was prepared to look in on the investigation that you are conducting, Inspector, does not mean that I need your assistance in the Carson investigation in return, does not mean that I can condone your pumping my officers, does not mean that I want you poking your nose into an enquiry which I'm conducting!'

'Superintendent!' The chief constable's tone was hard.

'No, sir!' Simpson, with a furious shake of his head was determined to have his say. 'You called in the Mets, and Chief Inspector Crow is handling his investigation. Fine. If he wants to run to me, again, fine. But I know my job, and I'm handling it as I see fit. I'm not having any irate parent like Carson interfering and I'm not having any damned superior-nosed character from the murder squad telling me how to run my business!'

Crow felt anger arising in his own veins at the injustice of the accusation.

'I am *not* interfering in your investigation at all, Superintendent! I have already attempted to explain just what I was doing—'

'Don't make me laugh!'

'Your emotions,' Crow said coldly, 'are as irrelevant to me as is your sense of humour. I have a job to do, and like you I'm doing it to the best of my ability. But I repeat, I was not interfering in your case!'

'Inspector!' The chief constable had heard quite enough. 'And Superintendent Simpson! I think this childish display has gone far enough. You are two senior officers. It is ridiculous that you should behave in this way. I think the whole thing should be taken no further.'

Simpson glared at Crow angrily.

'I've said my piece. I've nothing to add, anyway.'

Crow opened his mouth to make an angry retort, but bit back the words. He looked at the chief constable, but there was nothing to be read in the chubby face. Rogers wasn't taking sides. He was just ending a petty squabble.

Which was just what it had been, thought Crow as he lurched away unhappily outside Simpson's room. A pointless, petty squabble that had arisen largely because Simpson had in the first instance been touchy about the murder squad being called in at all. But it had soured relationships when they seemed to be improving.

Crow cursed. He'd wanted to talk informally with Simpson, raise the question of John Barnes's alibi, for there was something about the man that didn't ring true. But Crow could imagine Hugh Simpson's reaction if he mentioned it now. All right, it was Simpson's responsibility, the child murder. The hell with it; it wasn't for Crow to interfere.

He returned to the operations room to see Wilson staring thoughtfully at one of Lendon's red files. 'Sergeant Turner left this, sir.'

The file was marked *Barstow* in Lendon's bold hand. 'The Charlton file had nothing about Mrs Kent,' Wilson said, 'but this file does. Mrs Kent's been having it off with Dr Barstow, according to Charlton's report.'

'And Lendon didn't tell Mr Kent . . . We'd better see Dr Barstow and Mrs Kent tomorrow. Mmm . . . And I also want records to check on Michael Enson. I understand he and Lendon didn't get on.'

'I think you'd better look at this also, sir.'

'What is it?'

'It's the last will and testament of one Charles Lendon, deceased.'

Chapter 13

Just before lunch on Wednesday Maxwell, the assistant solicitor, stuck his head around the door in Cathy's room and pulled a face.

'I've just come from reception,' he said, elongating the grimace. 'One of your fans is out there, and says he'd like to have a word with you in Lendon's room.'

'Who is it?'

'Wilson. Detective-Sergeant, no less.'

The realization that it was the police rather than Mike slowed her pulse somewhat, and she felt almost relieved: she did not want to face Mike in the office. Or anywhere for that matter, at the moment, in the churning turmoil of her mind. She was vacillating, swinging wildly into indecision, unable to make up her mind or square her actions with her conscience or her conscience with her love. Yet the next moment the panic returned: the sergeant's visit could have something to do with Mike, after all, and that was almost as bad as having Mike out there in the office. Perhaps worse, in the long term.

Cathy took a quick look at herself in the mirror she extracted from her handbag. She looked reasonably presentable: reasonably only, for the sleepless nights were taking their toll and under her eyes were displayed tell-tale patches, dark beneath her light make-up. She snapped her handbag shut, went to leave it on the desk, and then had second thoughts. She decided to take it with her.

She took her time walking along to the room that had been Lendon's. The door was slightly ajar; she opened it and looked in. Wilson stood at the window, his stocky frame turned away from her, looking out into the street.

'Good morning, Sergeant. I gather you wanted to see me?'

Wilson turned quickly, a brief smile lighting up his serious face. He waved to a chair. 'Ah, hello, Miss Tennant. Just want a chat for a few minutes. Would you like to sit down?' She did as he suggested and he took Lendon's seat behind the desk. He had a folder in front of him.

'I'm sorry to bother you again, but there's just a few things we want a check on.'

'I'll do anything I can to help, Sergeant.'

He did not seem to detect anything untoward in her tone, which she herself felt was devastating in its insincerity. Her nerves screamed, Liar! even as she spoke.

'Well,' Wilson said heavily, 'we're still pursuing the line of enquiry we mentioned, about Mr Lendon's current girl-friends, and the possibility that he might have been meeting a woman on the afternoons unaccounted for. As you know, Inspector Crow regards your judgment as of some value, and he's suggested that I come around and put a few points to you, just in case you might be able to help us.'

She didn't believe it; it was too glib, and too nonsensical. Respect her judgment Crow might, but he would have other reasons for further questions, reasons other than those given by Wilson. She nodded carefully.

'How can I help?'

Wilson put his hands on the folder in front of him, and watched Cathy with careful eyes. 'We think that Lendon was meeting some woman, regularly, and in a rather clandestine fashion. We think that he saw her on the days when his presence in the office or elsewhere is unrecorded. The problem that's exercised us, obviously, is who is that woman? You did say that you had no idea?'

'None whatsoever. I suppose it's possible he was seeing someone, but I certainly don't know who it might be.'

'What about this Charlton business?'

Cathy shrugged non-committally.

'I can't help you on that matter. I met Mr Charlton, but I don't really know why he was employed by Mr Lendon.'

'Well, we now know why. A certain Mr Kent was interested in instituting divorce proceedings against his wife. He needed proof of adultery, so he consulted Mr Lendon about how he should go about it. Mr Lendon obtained the services of Mr Charlton in this connection and told Mr Kent that he'd be in touch in due course. Mr Charlton then proceeded to follow Mrs Kent, discreetly, and it would seem that he obtained some evidence that could have been useful to Kent. But . . . the information was never transmitted to Mr Kent. We wonder why.'

Cathy shook her head. She was puzzled. She could not understand why Wilson was telling her all this.

'I'm afraid I can't offer any explanation.'

'Can't you? We just wondered whether the name of Mrs Kent rang any bell for you.'

'It doesn't. I never heard Mr Lendon discuss her.'

Wilson looked doubtful.

'So you can't support the theory we have that Mrs Kent might be somehow involved in his murder.'

Cathy stared at Wilson's hands, fiat on the folder. She felt cold, suddenly. 'I don't understand.'

Wilson shrugged in an off-hand manner.

'Well, if Lendon suppressed the information he had from Charlton, could it not be that he might have got . . . er . . . rather interested in her? And could he not have met *her* during those afternoons? And could he not have gone to the Old Mill to meet her? It is after all a lovers' meeting place, isn't it? And if he did go there, couldn't she have killed him, or arranged to meet him there in order that someone else could kill him?'

'But I don't see why you——'

'You got the drift of all this, surely, from the Barstow file!'

'Barstow file?'

The genuine puzzlement in her tone must have been communicated to him, for there was a slight softening of his features. When she saw it she realized what was happening, in part. Wilson had told her all this because he guessed that she already knew what was in Lendon's files. The thought raised a swift query in her mind.

'If you're implying that I worked closely with Mr Lendon, why tell me all this now? I can assure you I know nothing about the Charlton-Kent affair, and I can also assure you that Mr Lendon was not the man to take me into his confidence.'

'In which case, you'll treat all I said as strictly between us, of course. After all, we've yet to follow up these enquiries. We just hoped that you might possibly be able to confirm our suspicions. Now then, another matter . . . we understand you're friendly with a Mr Michael Enson?'

She nodded unable to trust herself to speak. His sudden change in topic confused her, and the half-formed ideas about his motive for talking to her remained incapable of definition.

'Can you let us have his address?' Wilson asked. 'We have an address at the station, but we are under the impression that he's moved recently.'

'He's . . . he's now living over at Fenley, in a flat.' Cathy stumbled somewhat over the address as she gave it to Wilson. 'What do you want to see him for?'

'Just checking, that's all. You know, we have to follow up all lines of enquiry, and all possible enemies of Charles Lendon have to be interviewed.'

'Enemies?'

Wilson's eyes held hers steadily. They gave nothing away, conveyed no information. 'That's right, miss. We shall want to see Mr Enson tomorrow morning. I'll call this evening to tell him, unless you'd like to tell him. We'll want to see you, too, if you don't mind.'

In a daze, Cathy shook her head.

'I think that you'd better get in touch with him yourself. But what—'

'Well, if you can call around at the station tomorrow morning about eleven, we'd be very grateful, Miss Tennant. Just routine, you know.'

After Wilson had gone Cathy sat in her room for a long time, staring blankly at the papers on her desk. A vast confusion of mind prevented any focusing upon decision. She could see only a whirling kaleidoscope: Brian Philips, Mrs Kent, Mike, the letter in her handbag, Inspector Crow, Sergeant Wilson, her own guilt, her own conscience. And lying centrally in the kaleidoscope one clearly defined figure, the inert form of the dead Charles Lendon. Puzzled, confused, frightened and conscience-stricken, she could not think straight.

But Catherine Tennant wasn't a fool. She had a logical mind, a trained mind. Gradually she began to see things more clearly, began to understand the conduct of the man who had been with her. And she knew why he had come.

By the time she had grasped the significance of Wilson's visit the detective-sergeant had rejoined Crow at headquarters. Crow raised bushy eyebrows but Wilson gave his characteristic shrug, and shook his head.

'Mostly negative, I'm afraid. First, it's pretty obvious that she didn't know the contents of Lendon's files and she knows nothing about the Kent affair.'

Crow ran one hand over his bony skull and pursed his lips. 'I'd have been a little surprised, and somewhat disappointed too, If It had been otherwise.'

There was a disapproving note in Wilson's voice, when he added: 'In which case, sir, do you think it was wise to tell her of this line of enquiry?'

'I don't know. You see, as I explained to you, I'm convinced she knows more than she is yet prepared to tell. I hoped that if we showed her that we had someone under suspicion, this might jolt her conscience sufficiently to make her reveal what she does know, particularly if we seem to be implicating people who are innocent.'

'Well, she didn't come up with anything at all,' Wilson said with a dissatisfied grunt. 'And if I may say so, sir, if you think she has something she's holding back, I feel what we should do is have a go and get it out of her.'

Crow stood up and paced round the room with his hands behind his back. There was obvious sense in what Wilson said, and perhaps he was treating Cathy Tennant with kid gloves, using an unjustifiably psychological approach, and yet. . .

'I still feel we'd get no result that way. Did she respond satisfactorily to the statement that we wanted her and Enson in tomorrow?'

'I suppose she did. She went rather pale, and she was obviously frightened about something, and confused.'

Crow stared out of the window. There was a blackbird on the tree out there . . . blackbirds, crows, birds of ill-omen. He grunted unhappily.

'I'm sure she knows more than she tells us. I'm sure she's protecting someone. It could be Enson. And yet . . . I believe she's innately honest.'

It was a feeling only; Crow knew Wilson would be sceptical of that for supposition and 'feelings' could be fatal for a police officer on a murder case. No involvement; that was the rule.

'We'll see her and Enson tomorrow. Maybe the lid will blow off once they're both here.' Wilson watched impassively as Crow put on his raincoat. 'What about Barstow and Mrs Kent?'

'Get the dossier together and I'll look through it with you tonight. We'll have them both here tomorrow morning for questioning. Now, I've two calls to make.'

First, Mrs Alexandra Bell.

She was physically attractive but that was beside the point: he wanted her character, motivations, her will. She had used her body to buy security. That was a measure of her determination, but it didn't define its limits.

When he arrived at Lendon's house half an hour later there was no other car in the drive. Mrs Bell greeted him at the door; her smile was confident and friendly. She invited him in, her bearing displaying no trace of anxiety.

In the sitting-room she took a chair, folded her hands in her lap and sat with her back to the window. Her dark eyes were fixed on his. Crow looked at her and the thought of Charles Lendon came to him; the man could have done a lot worse than marry this woman. Crow brushed the thought aside: it was a triviality that only confused matters.

'I'm sorry to bother you again, Mrs Bell, but I'd really like to talk to you about a few points that we mentioned before. You told me that you came here as Lendon's housekeeper about seven years ago.'

She inclined her head gracefully.

'Now after you . . . after you became lovers, did Lendon continue in his . . . er . . . amorous wanderings?'

She smiled.

'I appreciate the delicacy of your phrasing, Inspector Crow, and I think I already know what's at the back of your mind. Perhaps I can put it like this. Although I said to you, perhaps in a weak moment, that I think Charles Lendon should have married me, we never really had the kind of relationship where I could be led to expect fidelity of him. I had certain expectations: I told you that he promised to look after me financially should he die before me, but marriage was not one of them. We became lovers, Charles and I, but this placed no chains on him. I was aware very shortly after we started our affair that he was seeing other women as well. He had a . . . well, a thing about it, really: every pretty woman he met presented a challenge to him and I think now that he was constitutionally incapable of letting an opportunity pass. In a word, he was a womanizer.'

'And this state continued?'

'You mean, did he continue to see other women? Oh yes. I wasn't his wife, I had no claims, no ties on him. He came and went as he pleased.'

'And you were not jealous.'

Alex Bell smiled again, warmly. She shook her dark head.

'I didn't say that. Of course I was jealous — at first. But I had the sense to say nothing and do nothing at the time, and later jealousy was an emotion I could not afford. So I discarded it. In a way, I suppose Charles was right, at the end, when he said that I knew my place.'

'So you had no strong feelings about the fact that he was conducting an affair just before he died with a woman from Canthorpe?'

'No,' she replied calmly, 'I did not. After all, nothing had changed. There was nothing new in the situation.'

'So you knew he was recently meeting some woman?'

'There was never a time when Charles was not involved in some affair or other! All right, you raise your eyebrows, so perhaps I do exaggerate. Nevertheless, there was nothing new in the situation.'

Crow studied his bony hands for a moment and then looked up to her dark, proud eyes. 'Did you know who the woman was?'

Alex Bell hesitated, then made a little moué and shrugged her shoulders helplessly. 'I didn't *know* . . . but I suspected that it might be .. a certain lady.'

'Would you care to give me her name?'

Alex Bell stared at him for a moment, as though considering whether her suspicions justified discussion.

'It makes little difference, I suppose, though I should emphasize that I only *suspected* a liaison, I didn't know for sure. There's a woman called Kent living in Canthorpe. . .'

'Mrs Gillian Kent.'

'That's right. I think it might have been her.'

'How did you come to think it was her?'

'One of Charles's less lovable characteristics was that he liked to talk about his women. Usually, this occurred after he had been with them; only occasionally, before he had managed to . . . to sleep with them. As far as Mrs Kent is concerned I only know that he had become interested in her. Then he stopped talking about her, which meant he could have achieved what he was after, or that his interests had moved in other directions. Towards that girl Tennant, for instance.'

'Cathy Tennant?'

The surprise in his tone made her look at him keenly. She shrugged.

'He talked about her a lot at one time. I wondered about it. I asked John . . . no matter. It came to nothing.'

Crow linked his fingers together, squeezed them, watched the fingers turn white as the pressure drove out the blood.

'We have to look for a woman in a case like this. Lendon went to the Old Mill, which is a lovers' trysting-place. He walked there, to meet someone? Knowing his predilections it was probably a woman. So he went there to meet a woman or to catch one in an activity of which he disapproved. The woman might have been his mistress, but meeting another man at the mill. Lendon was killed at that mill. The woman might have killed him; the man his mistress was meeting could have killed him. Who knows? Either is a possibility. You . . . you, of course, were asleep on your bed when Charles Lendon was walking up to the mill.'

There was an ironic gleam in her eyes when she answered him.

'As I told you, Inspector. But I fear there is no one who can verify that statement.'

'Then perhaps it was another woman . . . perhaps the . . . the woman he was interested in, or another. We'll find out in the long run. But there's one thing that doesn't seem to fit the theory that he was meeting a woman. You said he seemed preoccupied, nervy. Was that consonant with the excitement of a meeting?'

'No. If he had been meeting a mistress he would have been quite calm, and deliberate, and self-possessed. He was,' she added drily, 'a confident and very transparent man on such occasions.'

'Which means that the more probable theory is the one which suggests he was trying to catch someone out, or was meeting someone on a quite different matter?'

'The choice is yours, Inspector.'

He nodded, and rose suddenly, towering over her. She looked up at him with brilliant eyes, and again he was aware of the deliberate sexuality that she exuded. He returned her glance and with equal deliberation coldly phrased his words so as to strip away the affectation and the façade. 'Mrs Bell . . . when you came to Lendon, seven years ago, what *exactly* did he promise you?'

Something flickered in the depths of her dark eyes. It was gone before he could define the emotion it presented, but in a sense it confirmed his suspicions as to her cold control.

'He said that he would look after my financial problems while he lived and while we were together, and he said that if he died before me he would leave this house to me, together with an annuity which would leave me reasonably well situated.'

'Did he make these last promises freely, or did you pressure him into them?' There was a hint of mockery in her voice when she replied.

'Let's say that I used such powers of persuasion as were available to me at the time, bearing in mind that we had yet to become lovers.'

Crow did not return her smile. Seriously, he said: 'Did you know that he had made a will?'

'I did. He deposited it at the bank, I understand. I've been expecting them to arrive any day, as executors—'

'He didn't leave the will at the bank. His will was here, among his papers. The bank officials are not acting as his executors.'

Again something moved, deep in her eyes. He caught it now, an animal glint, a sense of danger. She was sitting very still.

'You found his will, then?'

'We did.'

They were both silent. It was the fact of his silence which finally drove her into the open.

'And?' There was a harshness in her voice now, and the warm full tones had gone. Crow regarded her steadily: her deliberate sexuality had evaporated. She was a hard, resourceful woman, strong of mind and will and body, and he caught a hint of her ruthlessness in the passionately fierce gaze she directed at him.

'You must understand my position, Mrs Bell. When we came across that will I was in a difficult situation. I had no right to look at it, and it should have been handed immediately to the executors. Indeed, I shall do that now, as soon as possible. Today, in fact. Nevertheless, I am also conducting a murder investigation, and I felt it necessary that I should look at the contents of the will, in case it gave me any further lines of enquiry to follow. So I looked, and I found something very surprising. But you will appreciate that I cannot give you the details . . . that will be for the executor obtaining probate.'

'You've read his will,' she said in a gritty voice, 'but you are not prepared to tell me what it contains?'

'That's right. On the other hand, I see no reason why I should not inform you that in spite of your expectations you are *not* the main beneficiary under that will!'

Chapter 14

'I don't really see how I can help you.'

Arthur Tennant was thickset and ruddy. He wore a grey shirt, tweed jacket and grey flannel trousers. From the width of the turn-ups Crow supposed the trousers to have been bought quite a few years previously. He slumped now in an easy chair in the sitting-room of the small bungalow where he lived, and he clenched an old briar pipe between his teeth, tamping at the tobacco with a yellow-stained finger as he watched Crow carefully with heavy pouched eyes. There was little of him in Cathy, physically, thought Crow, not her sharpness, nor her quick perception. There was a peasant quality about Tennant's hands, broad and thick-nailed, and the stolidity of his features was matched by the heavy complacency of his body. He was a comfortable man, and yet there was an edge of nervousness about him that put Crow in mind of an old, wary pike, watching the bait swim into vision. For the moment, Tennant was holding back, awaiting developments.

'Well,' the inspector said, 'you'll appreciate that when a murder investigation of this kind starts we have to follow up all sorts of avenues of enquiry. One of the most tiresome chores, and one which has to be done in spite of the largely negative results it produces, is the general interviewing of all who might have some connection with the dead man.'

Tennant tamped at the tobacco in his pipe. 'I still don't see where I fit in.'

'It's like this.' Crow remained patient. 'Your daughter worked for Lendon. Now Lendon is dead. You'll appreciate that it's our job to discover precisely what relationship existed between Lendon and the people in the office, and all the people who had social contact with him.'

'Relationship?' Tennant spoke quickly, and with a curious twitch of his eyebrows. 'Just what do you mean by that?'

Crow waved a lean hand diffidently.

'How well people knew Lendon, whether they met him regularly and so on. . .' He paused. 'Was that your wife?'

Crow was nodding in the direction of the photograph on the mantelpiece. It showed a young woman in a long cotton frock. She was squinting into a bright sun, and there was little to be made of her features, but the set of her head and her stance as she faced the camera certainly reminded Crow of Cathy Tennant.

'Ay,' Arthur Tennant said in a soft voice. 'That was my wife — Cathy's mother.'

'I can see Cathy in her.'

'You can? Ay, they are very alike. Cathy took very much after her mother. You know, as she grew up I could see the resemblance. You see, I watched Katie grow up, as I watched Cathy later. I was five or six years older than Katie and I was aware of her, you know? Aware of her sort of blossoming in her teens.'

'You knew your wife a long time before you were married?'

'Oh yes, a long time. We grew up in the same village. Grew up together, and there was a sort of understanding grew up between us too, but I never pushed things, not until she was old enough to know and understand and make up her own mind. When she did that, made up her mind I mean, we got married. We . . . we weren't married long . . .'

'What happened?'

'Katie died.' Tennant shrugged. 'She died when Cathy was born. Funny thing, really. When Katie died in childbirth and I saw that little mite in her blankets I thought that I'd call her the same name, Katherine, you know, but the registrar he got it spelt wrong and it came out Catherine. So it was Cathy.'

Tennant remained slumped back in his chair, and watched the blue smoke curl up from the pipe. He was silent for a moment and Crow left him to his memories, briefly. At last, with an apologetic smile, Tennant glanced at Crow and said:

'You must forgive me. You'll not want to know the story of my short marriage or the tale of Cathy growing up.'

'On the contrary, I would, for I have no little regard for your daughter. She's a bright girl. She has a rare judgment. When did she decide that she wanted to read law?'

Tennant leaned forward; he was obviously only too pleased to launch himself on the subject of his daughter, and his affection for her was plain.

'Well, I don't know that it ever happened just like that. As you probably know, I'm a woodwork master up at the grammar school and I knew the value of a good education. Cathy went to the school and I knew from my colleagues that she was bright. They wanted her to go to university and so did I, but she wasn't keen for some reason. I think she felt she wanted to get out, do a job of work. Anyway, we discussed it, and she didn't seem to know what she wanted to do, and I pointed out that if she were to read Law it'd be a good idea.'

'So you wrote to Lendon.'

'That's right,' Tennant said after a slight hesitation.

'How well did you know him?'

'How do you mean?'

'The question is simple enough.'

'I didn't know him very well.'

Crow raised his bushy eyebrows. 'You surprise me.'

Tennant's pouched eyes glared at his pipe as he tamped it with a darting finger. 'I don't know why you're surprised, Inspector.'

'Well, if you say you knew him only slightly, why is it that he named you as the executor to his will?'

Tennant froze. Something new lay in his eyes now, an expression of real fear. 'His executor? Me?'

'You are named as his first executor — and you didn't know?'

'I . . . I . . .'

'It's usual for an executor to be asked for his consent so to act before the will is drawn.'

'He didn't ask me!'

'And you weren't friends?'

'Never!'

There was a violence in the answer that gave Crow the hint he needed to confirm his suspicions. But he had to be sure.

'Tell me . . . is your daughter a *good* girl?'

The implied sneer in his tone brought Tennant from his chair. His face began to mottle in anger.

'What the hell do you mean?'

'It's quite simple. Is Cathy a good girl — in the old-fashioned sense of the word?'

Tennant was shorter than the inspector but he stepped forward, his head raised belligerently and his fists were clenched.

'Are you suggesting—'

'You must have heard about Lendon's reputation,' Crow said mildly. 'I'm just asking you whether your daughter might have become his mistress. Otherwise—' He glanced at the papers in his hand—'perhaps you could give me one good reason why the lecherous Charles Lendon should have left the bulk of his not inconsiderable estate to her.'

Chapter 15

The following morning Crow and Wilson were seated in the interview room, reading through the files which Turner had left for their perusal. They included the material that Lendon had kept on Dr Barstow and Mrs Kent, and Crow was just finishing the papers that Simpson's constable had produced on Michael Enson's father when the chief constable entered the room after a perfunctory knock. Crow rose to greet him.

The chief constable's chubby face was serious as he looked up to Crow. He prodded the file he carried in his hand.

'I've got the papers that Charles Lendon kept on his partner Philips. This chap Philips, he wasn't one of the world's gentlemen, was he?'

'You could put it like that, sir.' Crow permitted himself a faint smile.

'Well, it looks as though Lendon more or less drove Philips into signing over his share of the firm; at least, it looks that way from the account you included of the interview you had with him, and in a way it was Philips's own fault; indeed he could have got worse and ended up struck off the roll. And he did agree to leave the firm; still, there's not much that can be done about that. I imagine Lendon would have been too much of a lawyer to make the agreements with Philips less than watertight. The other stuff, of course, we're still very much concerned with.'

'You mean the company matters?'

'Mmm. I've had a word with our legal gentlemen and they've asked for the file to be sent up: it looks very much to me as though a prosecution will have to be mounted. There's certainly been some sort of shenanigans going on, and Philips looks up to his neck in it. I think it'll have to be followed through.'

The chief constable peered quizzically at Crow, and puffed out his round cheeks. 'Where does it all leave Philips as far as you're concerned?'

'With regard to the Lendon enquiry? Well, sir, we're not sure yet.' Crow had no desire to offend the chief constable, but he was not prepared to go into details concerning the investigation, not at this stage in the proceedings.

'I'm afraid that Mr Philips must remain on our list of suspects: he would seem to have had the motive for removing Lendon, he certainly disliked and feared him, he did have a quarrel with him, and his account of his whereabouts on that evening is unsubstantiated. I don't think we can take him at face value, even though he seems colourless and indeterminate.'

'You think he might have acted violently at the Old Mill?'

'It's a possibility.'

'Mmm. By the way, any trouble with the press?'

'I gave a short press conference this morning at ten. The usual stuff. They'll be back, no doubt.'

'You can count on that! All right, I'll get this Philips file sent on. The gentleman will be hearing from us.'

Once Rogers had gone Wilson asked whether they should proceed with the interviewing, but before Crow could answer there was a tap on the door and Detective-Sergeant Turner appeared.

'I thought you'd better see this at once, sir.'

Crow took the sheet of paper and read it slowly. It was a statement from a man living on the council estate near Lendon's home.

'Wilson, I believe I'm right when I say that Mrs Carson corroborated her husband's account of his movements on the night Lendon died?'

'That's right. They were both at home.'

Crow's voice was sad.

'According to William Stevens of Pavick Street, on the night Lendon died Stevens passed the time of evening with James Carson not two hundred yards from the Bear Inn, where Stevens had been drinking. Turner, get me a map, will you? Not the chief superintendent's, if you please!'

Crow stared thoughtfully at Wilson.

'I must be getting old. Time was when I instinctively knew when a man was lying. A man like Carson, anyway. But if Stevens is right, both Carson and his wife have lied.'

He didn't enjoy the thought. He liked them both; he had been sorry for them. His judgment had been clouded by compassion; he had too easily and too swiftly accepted what they had to say.

At times this job could be hell.

Turner came into the silence of the room with the map in his hand. Crow spread the map on the table and his bony finger traced the distance from the Bear Inn to the Old Mill.

'About a mile. Carson could easily have walked it in the time available.' 'But why should he walk across to the Bear after killing Lendon?'

'Assuming he did kill him, perhaps he was thinking of fixing an alibi. Clumsy. Perhaps he'll have an explanation. Meanwhile, we'd better get on with these others. We'll start with Mrs Kent and Dr Barstow.'

When they came into the room they avoided contact and they didn't look at each other. It was a curious situation: they'd been lovers, Crow knew, and yet they kept up this pretence of being virtual strangers even though she had been a patient of the doctor's.

'You'll know why I've asked you here.'

'On the contrary!' Barstow's reply was swift and harsh. 'We've no idea what you want. If it's anything to do with the Lendon murder I can't imagine why we're here. In any event, I think we should have legal representation at once.'

'If you feel you're on such insecure ground, in spite of the fact that this is merely a preliminary enquiry, by all means call a solicitor. Here's the phone.'

Crow waited, staring at Barstow. The doctor was a handsome man, broad-shouldered, dark-haired, carefully dressed. His eyes were rather fine, his mouth a little sensual, a little weak. And Mrs Kent . . . slender, tense, as anxious as Barstow, she was unable to hide her feelings or control her emotions. This could be one of the reasons why they found themselves here now. The lovely brown-eyed Mrs Kent might have let herself love too deeply for Dr Barstow's comfort. He might have wanted the excitement of an affair, but not the professional consequences.

A flush arose above Barstow's collar as the silence lengthened. The quick glance he directed at Mrs Kent suggested to Crow that the doctor certainly was laying the blame at her door. He nodded.

'So you decide against legal representation. All right, I'll go right ahead. I've information which suggests that Charles Lendon developed more than a passing interest in Mrs Kent. Perhaps you could give me details.'

Mrs Kent seemed to freeze momentarily, but she reacted swiftly enough, with a look of utter disbelief, when Barstow snapped:

'I don't see what that has to do with me!'

Crow regarded him carefully then turned to Gillian Kent. 'Mrs Kent?'

She seemed unable to speak. Her large, beautiful eyes flickered from Crow to Barstow and back again. Barstow was aware of her glance but refused to meet it and his hands gripped the side of his chair, fiercely, as he glared stonily at Crow's desk. Crow waited, then said:

'Mrs Kent's husband asked Lendon to place a watch on his wife to obtain evidence for a divorce. He engaged Raymond Charlton; the private enquiry agent duly reported to Lendon. The solicitor never passed the gist of that report to Kent. Instead, he told Kent that Mrs Kent had committed no improprieties. Yet Lendon's own files show quite clearly a liaison between Mrs Kent and Dr Barstow. The details were kept in a file on Dr Barstow, and were in fact duplicated in Charlton's own files kept at his home.'

Barstow had crumpled. His eyes were glassy, his fingers relaxed. He was a frightened man. Mrs Kent was unable to drag her eyes from him and her features were distressed. She put out a hand, but he seemed hardly aware of her. He was, thought Crow sourly, thinking about a medical career that was drifting away from him forever. Crow himself had other matters to think about.

'What I want to know is this. Lendon had evidence connecting you two as lovers. He was acting for Mr Kent. Yet he suppressed the information. Why?'

Silence greeted his question. Gillian Kent was still staring at Barstow; the doctor's gaze was still averted. He was trembling slightly, but otherwise he might not even have heard Crow's question.

'All right,' Crow continued with heavy patience, 'I'll put it like this. Charlton followed you two to your assignations, often it would seem at . . .' he consulted the papers '. . . at Rains Point. It is quite obvious that he had enough information to more than satisfy Mr Kent. Charlton handed this material to Lendon about last

November. Lendon paid Charlton's fees and that was that as far as Charlton was concerned. More than this of Charlton's part, we don't know. But after Charlton tendered his report there is a gap, a period when nothing seems to be happening. That period ends when Lendon suddenly writes to Kent, telling him that there is nothing to report. What I want to know now, is this: why the delay? And what happened to make Lendon write in this manner to Mr Kent?'

Gillian Kent turned her head towards Crow; she seemed about to say something, but bit her lip. Barstow still sat staring at the floor. Crow waited patiently. The silence grew around them like a physical thing, pressing in on them, and it was Gillian Kent who finally found the strain intolerable.

'Oh, for God's sake, Paul, we'll have to tell them!'

Barstow came alive. His handsome eyes flared angrily and he turned on the woman at his side.

'Shut your damned mouth, you fool! Can't you see they still know nothing?'

She started back in her chair as though struck in the face, but Barstow appeared not to notice. He was completely wrapped up in his own thoughts, his own problems, and whatever part Gillian Kent had once played in his calculations she played no part now: Barstow was fighting on his own and if her interests clashed with his, she would have to go by the board. Perhaps, at that moment, Gillian Kent realized this also: Crow gained the impression it had been something that had lain at the back of her mind during the last few days and Barstow's coolness towards her now only confirmed a suspicion. It was time to push the boat along a little, he thought; with his lip curling slightly in distaste Crow tossed the file across towards Barstow.

'If you think I'm bluffing, Dr Barstow, take a look for yourself. I want answers and I can call your bluff. If you don't provide answers, then I put the worst interpretation on your silence. And very damaging it will be, too.'

'What do you mean?' Barstow stared at the file as though unwilling to read it. His lips twitched nervously.

'Simply this. At the moment there's enough detail in that file to get you into deep trouble. It shows that you have been having an affair with a woman who was also your patient, and a married woman. You took advantage of your professional position. It's enough to get you struck off the medical register. That's what's worrying you at the moment. Forget that worry: there's not a thing you can do about it, now. Think about the next cause of anxiety.'

Barstow raised his head. Gillian Kent was still watching him with eyes that stared as though she were seeing him for the first time, through eyes unclouded with love. Barstow seemed hardly aware of her presence; a palpable nervousness oozed from his pores, and his handsome face was pale.

'What anxiety?'

'The anxiety you should be feeling at the thought that you, and Mrs Kent here, could have a murder charge to answer.'

'Murder!' Barstow gasped. Mrs Kent turned her head quickly towards Crow as the inspector continued:

'Yes, murder. Wasn't Lendon putting pressure on you? Wasn't he threatening to expose you? Couldn't you have killed him, to prevent him telling the world about your affair? Where were you, Barstow, the night Lendon died?'

'I . . .'

Barstow's eyes flickered towards Gillian Kent. Their glances met, and held, and as Crow saw the beseeching look in Barstow's eyes he felt his stomach churn unpleasantly. But for Gillian Kent everything snapped at that look. It was almost the first time he had recognized her presence and it was to plead with her to lie for him. It was more than her pride could stand. With a cold deliberation she said:

'No. Dr Barstow was not with me on the night Charles Lendon died.'

Barstow's eyes widened and he opened his mouth to protest. The protest died as he saw the expression on her face. He shook his head.

'I . . . I was out. I was worried, I took a drive up in the hills, and I walked, I don't know how long I walked. Hell, I just can't remember, I'm all confused. Gillian. . .'

'He was not with me,' she replied calmly to Crow. She was suddenly over a hill, past a barrier she had been unable to cross. 'We hadn't met in about three weeks, or a month.'

Crow nodded. 'I see. But Lendon was pressing Dr Barstow?'

'No. He wasn't.'

Crow caught the quick, uncomprehending glance that Barstow threw in her direction. The inspector regarded Mrs Kent: she was sitting very straight, and there was a flush on her cheek. She seemed to have a complete disregard for the effect her words might have on the man on her right and Crow felt that he understood her reaction. She was accepting an inevitable situation, the fact that Barstow was more concerned about saving his precious career than he was in thinking of her.

'You say I'm wrong in suggesting that a motive for murder would lie in Lendon's pressure upon Barstow?'

'Not wrong. Half right only.' Gillian Kent's face was stiff, her brilliant eyes hard. 'You see, the price for release of the pressure *had already been paid.*'

Wilson raised his head to look at her. Crow suddenly felt cold. Gillian Kent's face was expressionless. The two policemen almost involuntarily looked towards Dr Barstow, but his face told them nothing except that he seemed as puzzled as they.

'Perhaps, for the sake of the record, you'd better tell us what happened,' Crow said. Wilson bent over his pad.

'It's quickly told,' Gillian Kent replied with her head held proudly. 'I fell in love with Paul Barstow and I thought he loved me. It accounts for my conduct later. We had an affair. We knew nothing about Charlton's enquiries, we thought no one knew the truth about us until, out of the blue, Charles Lendon visited me. Then he saw Dr Barstow, and gave him rather more detail than he had furnished me with. There was silence for almost two weeks, during which time . . . Dr Barstow became ever more anxious. Then he asked me to go to see Lendon, plead on his behalf, explain we were in love. I didn't want to go . . . but I did. And received Lendon's proposition.'

She paused, faltering slightly, before continuing in an emotionless tone.

'Lendon told me he admired me, and said that exposure would destroy Dr Barstow's career. He said that Dr Barstow would be saved if I agreed to his suggestion. Lendon promised that he would write to my husband and tell him there was no evidence of a liaison, provided . . . provided I agreed to become Charles Lendon's mistress.'

Crow's glance shifted towards Dr Barstow. The man was sitting upright, glaring at Mrs Kent in a wild incomprehension. It was backed by a nervous fear that suddenly made his hands shake.

'I refused,' continued Mrs Kent. 'Lendon seemed not the slightest abashed. I formed the impression that he was not seeking a permanency: he desired me, and this was a way of satisfying his desire. I think he also found the method of pursuit satisfying in itself, it gave him a kick of some sort to put pressure on me, and humiliate Dr Barstow. It was like a game to Lendon. I received several telephone calls from him . . . I was beside myself with fear and anxiety . . . but in the end, one night . . .'

'Gillian!'

Barstow's voice was hoarse and he sat stiffly, his hands clenched in his lap. Mrs Kent paused and for just one moment her resolve crumbled. Then she rallied again and continued.

'I went to Lendon. I slept with him, eventually.'

Crow heard Wilson's involuntary indrawn breath, but he was watching Barstow's face. The man's mouth seemed to crumple, like a child taking an undeserved beating.

'Dr Barstow didn't know.' Gillian Kent's tone was now quite impassive, as though spoken in a dream. 'But his anxiety had cut me to the quick, and his unhappiness so upset me that when Lendon suggested this short affair I finally gave in. I met Charles Lendon several times. He took me to dinner. He was courtesy itself: he didn't rush things. We . . . we finally slept together on about five occasions.'

'Can you give me dates?'

'I can. Our later meetings took the form of afternoon visits to my flat. The last occasion was . . . was the day he died.'

Crow glanced significantly towards Wilson. They now knew where Lendon had been spending his time during the periods not accounted for in his diary. Crow hesitated. 'And that evening? The night he died?'

'I was at my flat. Alone. Trying to telephone Dr Barstow. I couldn't get through to him. I . . . I was desperately unhappy. Next morning I heard that he . . . Charles Lendon was dead, and with an immense relief I ran round to see Dr Barstow. I didn't catch him in then, but when I finally met him at his surgery he seemed in no way pleased to see me. I told him I thought that now everything would be all right for us. But he guessed that . . . that this would happen, that the information would come into your possession. Me . . . all I could think of was that my sleeping with Lendon had achieved nothing, after all. It was all going to come out in any case.'

Gillian Kent's eyes were blurred now, glistening with tears that lay at the back of her lids. But she sat with her head high and Crow reasoned she had some cause for pride: she had sacrificed herself to Lendon to save Barstow.

'Do you have anything to add?'

Barstow shook his head. He seemed stunned as he continued to stare at Mrs Kent. Her eyes avoided his as though she feared to see contempt in them. There was no contempt, only the dawning of a realization. Crow sensed that Barstow had not known how deeply Gillian Kent had loved him — now he knew.

'I shall have to ask you for a statement nevertheless. Sergeant Wilson will take it from you.'

Mrs Kent sat with her head lowered and Barstow put out his hand. The weakness had left his mouth and there was a determined glint in his eyes. Crow had seen it happen before, but never as clearly as this. The man who had taken, and indulged his sensual whims, was suddenly accepting his responsibilities. As his hand touched hers Mrs Kent looked up and she too saw what lay in his eyes.

Crow rose to his feet and walked towards the door. Time now to see Cathy Tennant: he wasn't looking forward to the interview. But at least, he thought, Lendon's death had achieved something. Barstow might well be struck off the medical register, but he had in a sense found his own manhood. The humiliation that Gillian Kent had suffered for him would be something he could never turn his back on.

Love, Crow thought, could be a painful experience. It had been for Mrs Kent, and now Barstow was feeling the birth pangs. But Crow's guess was that it would work out well.

He was not so confident of the result of the interview he was about to conduct.

Chapter 16

'Take a seat, Miss Tennant.'

She had changed since Crow first met her. Her eyes were evasive, and shadowed as though she had spent more than one sleepless night. She seemed to have taken little trouble with her appearance, and her hands displayed an uncharacteristic nervousness and instability. Crow wondered whether it was merely anxiety occasioned by the fact she had information that she was holding back, or whether there were other causes. Arthur Tennant would not have spoken to her: Crow had demanded the promise from him before he left, so she could hardly be aware of the contents of Lendon's will. Unless Lendon himself had told her previously.

Crow rose to his full height and stretched. He smiled apologetically at Cathy. 'Sometimes I think I should have been a farmer. Sitting behind a desk never did suit me. My joints creak after a bit.'

There was no answering smile from the girl. She sat on the edge of her seat and she did not meet his eyes. Wilson remained quietly at the other table. Crow eyed him briefly, went back behind his desk and levered himself into a reasonably comfortable position. He placed his bony hands on the desk and leaned forward sympathetically.

'Don't you think that it's time you told us?'

The way her eyes leapt to his reminded him of the image of a startled fawn at the advent of the dogs. She was frightened . . . more, she was terrified. But not for herself, he was sure. For herself Cathy Tennant would not display such naked panic.

'Ever since we first met,' Crow said gently, 'I've had the feeling that you have information to impart to us, but for reasons of your own . . . loyalty, perhaps . . . you've kept that information back. I've waited, as Wilson will tell you, in the belief that your own common sense would finally tell you that you must impart it to us. You haven't yet done so. Why not now, Miss Tennant?'

She shook her head in simulated bewilderment. She was too honest to be a good actress.

'I don't know what you mean.'

'Come off it, Cathy. You don't mind me calling you that, Cathy? I have a regard for your intellect: I'd be somewhat distressed if you didn't pay me the same compliment. I *know* that you're holding something back.'

Again she shook her head. Her expression remained blank.

'I'm afraid I've nothing to tell you. I just don't know what you're talking about.'

Crow sighed, but remained gentle.

'Look, Cathy, let me put it to you like this. Charles Lendon was murdered, quite brutally, at the Old Mill. You knew him. I think you respected him. There don't seem to be many who have a good word to say for him, but I've not heard you criticize him. You took him with his faults . . . you judged him by his conduct towards you. Now, bearing that in mind, do you think it's right that you should do anything to shield his murderer?'

He saw that he had hit the right note. Her panic increased, but she was still shaking her head.

'I'm not hiding anything, it's got nothing to do . . . I don't know who murdered him.'

'But you do have information which might have some bearing on the case. Something you've kept back from us.'

'I don't, I don't. I have no information that—'

'It's Michael Enson, isn't it?'

'What?'

He had shocked her; her worried eyes were meeting his for the first time and she was sitting bolt upright. Two bright spots of colour burned in her cheeks.

'I think that the information you have is damaging to your young friend Enson. That's why you've not given it to us. It's the only explanation for your conduct. It must concern someone of whom you're fond: I've seen Arthur Tennant and it doesn't involve him. There's only one other person close .to you, and that's Enson. And I think you know something about him, something to connect him with what happened at the Old Mill. You know he had a grudge against Lendon—'

'Grudge? What grudge?'

'—and I know you must have quarrelled with him over something. That's why you ran away from him in the woods . . .? That's it, isn't it, why you've not seen him just recently — we're not blind fools, Cathy — and that's why the knowledge that you're keeping something from us is burning you up. You're caught out in conflicting loyalties — towards Lendon, and towards us, and towards Michael Enson. But it can be resolved only one way, Cathy, even if it hurts. Our way. It's the only way in the long run.'

He could see the agonizing struggle that she was having with her conscience. The pain that it caused her was reflected in her face. But even as he saw the pain he knew that he had lost the battle right from the start. She could not tell him the truth: it would cost her too much in the telling. Her sense of what was right was inevitably being overridden by her love. He glanced across to Wilson and read the same thought in the Yorkshireman's expression. She wasn't going to speak. Her next words only served to emphasize it all.

'I really can't help you, Inspector.'

Her voice was quiet, and almost resigned in quality.

It was as though she had reached a final decision. But for Crow it couldn't be final; he had to make her go back on that decision. And there was only one way, only one method. The direct and brutal method. He stared at her coldly for a long moment and then, with a deliberately induced harshness, he changed his tack abruptly.

'Did it ever occur to you that Charles Lendon loved you?'

He had the painful satisfaction of seeing the shock of the question drive out what colour was left in her face.

'I. . .what on earth makes you . . .'

'I repeat: did you know that he loved you? Did he ever give you cause to think so?'

'No! Never!'

'What was his attitude towards you?' She was flustered, and annoyed. She shook her head in angry desperation.

'His attitude? It was . . . well, it was ambivalent.'

'Ambivalent? What the hell is that supposed to mean? Was he fond of you?'

'Well, yes, I suppose he was in a way, but—'

'How did he show it?'

'Well, the way he looked at me sometimes, and once in a while he would touch my shoulder as though . . . really, Inspector, I don't see what all this has to do with—'

Crow put up a hand; the fingers were thin and predatory, the gesture peremptory.

'Don't tell me my job, Miss Tennant. All I want from you is answers, not questions, or comments. You tell me you found Charles Lendon's attitude towards you ambivalent. On his side, at least, they were obviously clear-cut.'

She was eyeing him a little warily. She leaned forward in her chair, her face chased with emotions of conflicting puzzlement, curiosity and fear.

'Clear-cut? I don't know what you're driving at, Inspector.'

'Then I'd better spell it out for you, Miss Tennant. I take it that you were aware that Lendon had . . . shall we call it, an affection for you? But you were not, of course, aware that he intended leaving most of his estate to you.'

'*What?*'

Crow made no effort to repeat the statement. There was adequate testimony to the fact that she had heard clearly the first time. She was riveted to the chair, unable to move, her face expressive of complete surprise, shock and bewilderment. It was also testimony to the fact that she could not previously have known of the terms of Charles Lendon's will.

Some moments elapsed before Cathy recovered from her surprise. 'You . . . you can't be serious. You can't say that this was his intention—'

'His intention,' Crow replied with cold precision, 'and his action. You are the main beneficiary under Charles Lendon's will. He left little to anyone else, apart from an annuity to Mrs Bell, with whom he has been virtually living for the past seven years.'

Cathy looked stunned. She seemed incapable of comprehending the situation, but she made an effort to pull herself together.

'I can't believe it,' she murmured. 'I never thought . . . why could he possibly want to do that?'

'He also made Arthur Tennant his executor, to administer the estate and hand it over to you.'

She obviously found this information equally puzzling. 'But Dad hardly knew Charles Lendon, if he knew him at all. And Dad never told me that he was to be Lendon's executor.'

'For the simple reason that he himself did not know until this week.'

Cathy was completely lost now, and vulnerable. Crow had delivered the opening cannonade: it was time to press home the advantage, to break down her defences and emphasize the point, which Crow hoped would finally make Cathy see sense. He took a deep breath.

'I want to tell you a story now, Miss Tennant. An old story, twenty-five years old. A story about three people, living not far from here. One was a young girl: she was about eighteen, pretty, lively, a little vain perhaps, but what pretty girl at her age isn't? Ever since she was thirteen she'd been friendly with a young man five or six years older than she and it had become accepted that one day they would marry. When she was eighteen, they became engaged.'

Cathy was inattentive, only half listening: her mind was still spinning around the facts he had already given her.

'Her fiancé was a steady chap, he had a good job locally, and he was a dependable man. But he had always been around and he lacked glamour. Then she suddenly found just that.'

Cathy was nervous. She opened her mouth to speak but Crow forestalled her.

'Please hear me out. This young girl knew little of men, and when her cousin came to stay briefly with the family she was overcome by him. He was in his thirties, handsome, capable, worldly, intelligent. He swept her off her feet, she was wildly in love with him, a young, new love, and he took advantage of the situation. He seduced her. They became lovers.'

She was listening to him now. Stories of love for lovers were always of fascination.

'She was mistaken about him. Perhaps she believed the things he said, perhaps she read more into the situation than she should have done. Whatever it was, it became quite obvious he intended no permanency. He tired of her and left the area. Within two weeks of discarding her, breaking off the affair, the girl found herself pregnant. It's impossible to say what she felt, or what motivated her but she ran away from the village, took a job in another town . . . and later, when the time came, she had her baby in a nursing home. It was stillborn.'

Crow paused. Cathy was wide-eyed.

'She might have stayed there, alone, unhappy, but her fiancé sought her out. One can look only with considerable regard upon that man. He sought her out, persuaded her to marry him. And I think he might have made her forget her unhappiness, for they had three years together before she died, in childbirth.'

Cathy was an intelligent girl; Crow had her attention and saw the flicker in her eyes. 'The child was a girl. He brought her up, lavished affection on her, and she grew into a beautiful woman. But as she grew she became more and more a drain on him financially, and though he had a good job he wasn't wealthy and he wanted the best for her. He wanted her settled in a profession and when he received a communication from a solicitor in Canthorpe it came as a surprise, but not an unwelcome one, for all its unpleasant associations.'

'Charles Lendon.' Her voice was quiet, and tense.

'Charles Lendon. The man who seduced his own cousin all those years ago now wanted to help in the education of his cousin's daughter.'

'But why? Why?' Crow shrugged.

'I think there were many conflicting reasons. Lendon knew about the stillborn child, the marriage of his cousin to Arthur Tennant, the birth of a daughter . . . you. Your father, well, I think he had hated Lendon all these years, but when Lendon wrote to him he agreed to talk. Your father told me that Lendon said he'd look after you professionally, bring you on in the firm. Tennant didn't believe Lendon when he said that this was his way of making up for the wrongs he had done his cousin, but then, there's no reason why Arthur Tennant should feel charitably towards Lendon.'

'What do *you* think?'

Crow looked at her passively. 'Is it important?'

'I . . . I don't know.'

She was confused, and Crow hated the fact that he had to use her confusion, but he had a job to do.

'Perhaps Tennant misjudged Charles Lendon. Perhaps Lendon was trying to make up for the wrong he had done his cousin, your mother, all those years ago. On the other hand, although he has left you his estate, that might have been dictated by the desire to hurt Mrs Bell. Who can tell?'

He paused, eyeing the girl carefully.

'There's one thing we do know. He became fond of you.'

'What do you mean?'

'You've told me his attitude towards you was ambivalent. He hadn't changed much over the years, he was still a roué, a womanizer, but perhaps he really did love your mother in his way. Perhaps he felt pangs of regret for his behaviour towards her, but whatever it was once you were with him at the firm did he not show an unusual attitude, for a principal, towards you? You were puzzled by the way he looked at you, touched you on occasions '

'You said he left me his estate.'

'That's right. Perhaps to hurt Mrs Bell. Or perhaps because he saw your mother in you. Or saw in you the daughter he could have had, but never did.'

She was shaking her head. It was all too much for her to comprehend and her own emotions were so confused that she was unable to think clearly. Crow continued to press her.

'So I want you to think about it all, Cathy. I want you to think about Charles Lendon and your mother, about your father, about the way they've all been bound up together during these years. Arthur Tennant hated Charles Lendon but he saw the sense in accepting Lendon's offer of a career for you, even though he doubted Lendon's motives. And Lendon left his estate to you, naming Tennant as his executor. All right, that's a cruel joke too, in view of Tennant's hatred of Lendon, but this was the sort of man Lendon was. The fact is, what are you going to do about it now?'

'Do? What do you mean?'

'Are you going to tell us the truth, tell us all you know or will you keep silence?'

'I . . . I don't know what you mean. There's nothing . . .' There were tears now, glittering like sunshine on a river and Crow knew that she was all but exhausted emotionally. But he could waste no time on sympathy, he could give her no time to live again the days she had spent in Lendon's company in his office, to visualise the way Lendon had looked after her, watched her, regarded her with pride. Crow had to attack, underline the half recognized emotions.

'I want you to think,' he said urgently, 'before you say another word. I want you to remember that Charles Lendon loved your mother. I want you to remember that in his own way he tried to make up for what he had done to her by bringing you into his firm. I want you to remember that in his own possessive, strange way he came to love you too, as a father loves a daughter — for that can be the only explanation of his attitude towards you. And I want you to remember the way he died, in agony, with a skewer in his heart. I want you to picture him coughing out his life, alone, at the Old Mill. And I want you to realize, and accept, that anything you hold back, any information you keep to yourself concerning his death will be a protection for the man who murdered . . . not just anyone, not a stranger, not just your employer. You're protecting the man who murdered Charles Lendon . . . a womanizer, a hard, selfish man, but a person who loved

165

your mother and who tried to atone for his treatment of her, through you!'

Cathy groaned and closed her eyes. Crow felt sorry for her. She would never know the truth about Charles Lendon. She would never be sure whether he had really tried to atone or whether he was indulging in a bitter joke at Arthur Tennant's expense, and at Mrs Bell's expense. But the doubts were there and they would always be there. Charles Lendon might have looked upon her as a man looks upon his daughter. He might have willed her his estate out of affection and love. They were doubts Crow fostered and used. He watched the girl as she put her head back on the chair, despairingly. Then without warning she lurched forward, throwing her hands up to her face. The tears came, violently. Crow nodded to Wilson and the sergeant left the room, to return a few minutes later with a cup.

'Tea,' Crow said apologetically, putting his bony fingers gently on Cathy's shoulder. 'Special; laced with whisky from Wilson's special bottle. Strictly against regulations.'

'I'm sorry,' Cathy said, sniffing. He knew she meant not only the tears, but everything. 'My handbag.'

At her nod Crow opened the clip. 'The letter, in the blue envelope.'

Crow read it quickly, then again, more slowly. At last he turned to the silent detective-sergeant beside Cathy. 'Tell the desk sergeant I'll want Enson brought in here in five minutes' time. Before that, I want you to take Miss Tennant home.'

Wilson nodded and left the room. Crow read the letter again. 'Where did you get this, Cathy?'

'It was pushed on top of the files in the cabinet in the anteroom.'

'You think Lendon must have intercepted it, then pushed it hastily in the filing drawer before leaving the office?'

'I . . . I imagine so. When I saw it I . . . I took it, because . . .'

'Was the envelope with it?'

'No. There was just the paper.'

'Was it Enson who was with you the night you came out of the woods and I met you?'

She nodded, despairingly, and he stared at her with compassion. Life could be hell when you were young, and love could be worse. He began to speak, but was interrupted by the violent opening of the door.

It was Wilson, shaken out of his Yorkshire taciturnity.

'It's Enson, sir. He's gone. He left headquarters not two minutes after Miss Tennant was brought in here.'

Chapter 17

The next ten minutes were hectic. Crow got in touch immediately with the operations room and had a call put out to all patrol cars in the town. A car was dispatched with Detective-Sergeant Turner to Enson's address and then Crow discussed the possible necessity for road blocks and checks to be made in and around Canthorpe. It wasn't going to be easy. In the discussion, Crow almost forgot Cathy.

When he returned to the interview room and saw her face he felt a rush of sympathy. The news had meant as much to her as it had to them: it was possible that Enson would have an explanation for his sudden disappearance from the precincts, but when allied to Cathy's presence at the station and the letter she had produced, Enson's action looked suspiciously like the flight of a guilty man. Crow and Wilson thought so, and Cathy's face told them that she was of the same mind.

'Before I get a car to take you home,' Crow said in a gentle voice, 'I should ask you: do you have any idea where young Enson might have gone? Is there any possible

'You think he's the one? For the Lendon killing?'

'It is a possibility.' The repetition emphasized Crow's caution. 'There are signs that—'

'Signs! Don't talk to me about bloody signs! That's all I've been getting on this Carson killing . . . signs, and not a real bloody track to follow. Eight weeks and we're where we damned well started. All those statements, all that paper-work and it's led only to three suspects cleared and not another thing out in the open.'

It was obvious that Simpson had not come in to discuss the Lendon affair: he was openly bringing in the Carson killing. Crow regarded the big superintendent dispassionately.

'You've had a house to house?'

'House to house and door to bloody door! Take a look in the ops room, Crow, and see the mountain of paper. And the press, hell, the press, I wish they'd get the hell out of it!'

'It'll crack,' murmured Crow.

'Or I will!' Simpson's tone was snappish. He relapsed into a moody silence, staring out of the window, and Crow watched him for a moment. He remembered the last occasion when he had spoken to Simpson: maybe it was the superintendent's lack of success that had caused him to fly into a rage then. The point was, Simpson had now come to Crow. The inspector took a deep breath.

'Do you mind if I ask you something?' Crow noted the stiffening of Simpson's shoulders and there was a truculence in the man's tones when he replied; nevertheless he invited Crow to pose his question.

'Go ahead.'

'I have no intention of interfering in your investigation, Superintendent, but I will ask you just this one question. Have you looked at John Barnes?'

The thick eyebrows frowned; the wary eyes held Crow. 'Barnes? Who . . . what's there about Barnes? We've nothing on him, so why do we look at him?'

Not an outright refusal, not a throwing back in Crow's teeth, simply a reluctance that could be accepted as part of the man's make-up. Crow grimaced.

'You know how it is in this job, Superintendent. It's part luck, part hard work and part intuitive experience. I'll come right out now and say that I have no positive, concrete reason for suggesting that you should look closely at Barnes, no evidence to point to his involvement. But I've met him and I've got a feeling—'

Simpson snorted, but Crow continued calmly:

'—I've got a feeling about the man. There's something *wrong* about him. He told me about the search for the little girl and he obviously felt something compulsive about it. He could no more have stayed away from that search than he could prevent himself from telling me all about it. I can't explain the impression he made upon me; all I can say is, just once before have I received such an impression and the man concerned turned out to be a psychopath.'

Simpson was staring at Crow with a contempt that he made no attempt to conceal. He snorted again. 'This sounds like a Mother's Corner magazine! Intuition! A *feeling* about the man!'

'That's what I said.' Crow's reply was quietly phrased, but underlined by stubbornness.

'You're an experienced officer and you can come out with guff like that,' Simpson said. 'It makes me ask myself what the hell we're doing these days. Intuition is for the birds.'

'You know better than that, Superintendent. You know as well as I that there are times when a man comes before you with a cast-iron alibi and yet you know in your bones he's as guilty as hell. It will have happened to you: yet you deny me the word intuition. Well, no matter. The thing is, I've told you now. I'd have done so earlier—'

'But you thought I'd regard it as meddling. All right, fair enough. But intuition, man, it's a load of poppycock and you know it.'

He scraped a horny hand against the rough stubble of his chin. He shrugged suddenly in capitulation.

'Still, I'll have to check it now. We'll have taken his statement and that of his sister, and checked it against others but . . . well, I'll settle for old wives for a few hours, hey?' He turned to go back but paused at the door as though about to add something. In the event he went out, without speaking. Crow knew their relationship wasn't sufficiently close for admissions of weakness.

Just before five-thirty Crow rang the Lendon office and spoke to Cathy Tennant. 'How are you feeling?'

'I've been busy, Inspector. It's helped. Have you found Mike yet?'

'No. You've heard nothing from him?'

'We've . . . we've not been in touch for days.'

Not since the night in the woods, Crow thought grimly.

'Inspector, I, don't want to sit at home all night; I can't face it. I'm thinking of going to see Mrs Bell. Did . . . did she expect much from . . . Lendon?'

Crow told her what Alex Bell had said about the arrangement she'd made with Lendon. Cathy was silent for a moment.

'I must see her,' she said suddenly. 'I can't let things stand like this. I can't accept everything from the estate. He . . . he was wrong, leaving so much to me. I must see her, tell her the house must be hers. I couldn't take it away from her . . . I must tell her, before she hears the details of the will from other sources.'

'It's up to you, Cathy.' He understood the other unspoken need that she felt. The need to make some contact, reach for something or someone that Charles Lendon had known and touched, possibly loved. She wanted to break through the barriers of her own experience and know Lendon as someone close to him had known him. The old, shadowy existence that he had had for her as an employer was no longer enough. She wanted to know more of him as a person.

'I think I'll go out there tonight. You have no objection?'

'There's no objection at this end, Cathy. But I say again, don't be too late home. It's been a rough day for you. You need rest. And Enson . . .'

'Yes?'

'When we find him, I'll let you know.'

She made no reply but he guessed that she would have appreciated the reasons that motivated him. After she rang off he prowled uneasily around the room for a while. Something bothered him. Nothing he could put a finger on. But the Enson situation bothered him, Cathy bothered him, and there was something else. Chords; chords on a piano, too many false chords. The whole investigation was out of tune: he knew it, but he could not detect where the tunelessness lay. He went down to the canteen for a cup of tea.

He was interested to note that, like himself, Simpson was staying late at HQ. Wilson took a break about six and Turner came in and out: the young detective-sergeant seemed to be in no hurry to leave. Crow brooded, hunched in his chair like a great black bird. He was aware of the simile that would be bandied about the station: he'd lived too long with it to be bothered by it. But he was bothered about *something*.

At eight-thirty the door opened suddenly and Simpson stood there with a sour expression. 'It's getting to look like no race at all.'

'I don't understand.'

'Your bloody intuition! Barnes was in the nursing home that night. There's an old porter who substantiates it . . . night and morning. So much for your theories!'

His heavy brows drew together.

retain the house, and make a gift of it to Lendon's mistress and housekeeper.

She sat in the bus and stared out of the back to the cold glittering surface of the road, marked darkly by wheels slashing along its surface. A heavy whitening frost had fallen and the night air caught at the throat with its sharpness. The headlights of a car far behind the bus rose and dipped and glanced along the distant curves, moving with care, making no attempt to pass the bus on the slippery road. It drove past only when Cathy alighted and walked towards Kenton Lane.

The hedge was tall to her right, the line of council houses black against the starlit sky. To her left stood the first scattering of timber that was Kenton Wood. Her shoes crunched loudly on the frozen surface of the lane, patched with tar macadam, hard-rutted, spiky with ice. Her breath moved ahead of her, drifting around her like a ghostly halo. A gleam of light flickered ahead. Charles Lendon's home.

The drive was empty. Cathy pressed the bell push and after a few moments lights sprang below and the door opened. Mrs Bell stood there in the doorway.

The light behind her accentuated her figure and Cathy got a quick impression of a tall, shapely woman with dark hair. Mrs Bell's voice was resonant and curious.

'Yes?'

'Mrs Bell?'

'That's right.'

'My name's Cathy Tennant.'

A brief pause, then Alex Bell stood to one side and asked Cathy in. She walked into the hallway of the quiet house and saw the heavy wood staircase with its polished used look, and she heard Mrs Bell say: 'Come in here. It'll be warmer.'

Mrs Bell switched on the electric fire in the sitting-room and as she did so Cathy noted the clean, strongly beautiful line of the woman's neck.

of anger and advancing years. The house waited around them, the clock ticked unhurriedly, and Cathy heard the other sounds, the creak of old timbers, the groans of an old house.

'You'd better go.'

Mrs Bell's voice was cold and flat.

'I'm sorry, Mrs Bell, and I want—'

'I said you must go. *Now.*'

Cathy's pulse quickened unaccountably. There was a violence in Alex Bell's manner that unnerved her.

'The back door is open.'

'The back door? Can't I—'

'*I said the back door!*'

Cathy stepped back a pace. She hesitated, then turned quickly and walked out of the room. She turned through the corridor to the kitchen and saw the back door. She reached for the handle and Alex Bell said just three words more.

'Goodbye, Catherine Tennant.'

The door handle twisted under Cathy's fingers and she was out in the cold glittering darkness, and the frost was on her burning cheek and the stars rode high.

Silence swept in behind her. Cathy stood against a tree at the back of the house and tears ran down her face. Not tears for her humiliation or pain, but tears for a dead man and for a love that had been no love but a bargain, and for a woman who in Charles Lendon's death lost self-respect and beauty and charm to become a symbol of cold hate.

The lights in the house went out. Cathy rubbed her hand against her face, and her nose was cold, and wet with tears. Blubbering like a kid. She sniffed, drew out a handkerchief and blew her nose. The house was dark.

Somewhere, a door slammed, with a light, yet not distant sound. Not an internal door, but another. The front door.

There was no wind, no rustle from the winter trees.

No moon. Just the cold, hard, glittering starlight, and the white frost and the dark etching of trees against sky. She remembered the sounds of Mike's body, forcing his way through Kenton Wood in pursuit of her, and she shivered.

Something crunched in the driveway.

Cathy raised her head. The darkness of the house lay to her left; the driveway waited silently ahead of her. Beyond was the lane and the path and the houses and the road. Cathy stepped forward hesitantly.

Frost crunching quickly and lightly, then silence. Had it been her own movement, or her imagination?

She could not be sure, but her heart began to beat more quickly again, where it had slowed in the seconds after her retreat from the house. Had Mrs Bell left the house . . . .. had that been the sound of the slamming door?

'Mrs Bell?'

Stupid. Silly. Frightened, like a little girl. The voice hung quavering in the cold night air and Cathy hated it for its weakness and its credulity and its fear. She shook herself, and walked forward confidently towards the drive and the frost crunched firmly beneath her feet. The side of the house loomed blackly up at her and to her left, and she walked past the front door and into the lane. The trees stretched sombre arms above her head, and in the faint starlight she saw the dark marks that her feet had made in the crisp frost on the pathway.

But even as she saw the other marks the torch flickered at her from the darkness, pinning her in its beam. It held her briefly, contemplatively, and then it was gone. Next moment Cathy's scream lanced the air as she made out the dark shape leaping towards her and heard the swift, sliding sound.

The breathing was harsh, and animal.

Chapter 20

Chief Inspector Crow stretched his long legs under the table, cupped his angular jaw within thin fingers and stared at the sullen face of Mike Enson, glaring at him from the chair in front of the desk. The young man was angry; but his anger was a compound of incomprehension, suspicion and fear. It was puzzling. Crow tapped the letter on the desk.

'So you deny writing this?'

'I've told you. I know damn all about it!'

'But the signature is yours.'

'It looks like my signature, I agree, but then my signature is hardly difficult to copy, is it?' Crow agreed drily. There was a curious, stereotyped immaturity about Enson's writing that in no way reflected the personality of the man before him. Crow sighed.

'All right. Let's go over the whole thing again. Just to get the picture straight, from my point of view as well as yours.'

Enson opened his mouth to protest but Crow overrode him.

'You became friendly with Cathy Tennant. You had no idea she was the object of Charles Lendon's interest and affection, though you did know she worked in Lendon's office. Not long after your association with Miss Tennant began, Lendon became aware of it. There is no doubt he would disapprove of it. You continued to see Miss Tennant, and one evening you had something of a quarrel, not serious, but upsetting, because she refused to marry you immediately. You then wrote her a letter which—'

'I said I wrote no damned letter!'

'-which suggested a meeting at the Old Mill. The terms you used were short and succinct.' Crow glanced again at the letter and read out:

"Darling,

I must see you tonight. Can you make it at the Old Mill, about eight? I'll be waiting there. Yours, Michael"

He looked up to Enson.

'But you miscalculated; you didn't expect Lendon to intercept the letter. You left it at the office and Lendon picked it up when he returned that afternoon, opened it, read it and stuffed it into a file. He left the office and drove to a lay-by where he sat for a while, brooding about your association with his cousin's daughter. He drove home, where his housekeeper noticed his preoccupation. It was then that he decided to do something positive about you. Cathy hadn't received the letter; she knew nothing about the assignation. But Lendon did, and he didn't take his car to the Old Mill: he wanted to surprise you, have it out with you, warn you off. He walked up there, and you were waiting. What happened then, Enson? Did you panic when you saw him? Or was it more premeditated? Did you see him coming and realize that here was a chance to revenge yourself upon the man you hated? Did you cast around, see the rusty skewer, pick it up and as he walked through the doorway, plunge it straight into his heart? Was that how it was, Enson?'

'I shall never understand,' Enson growled sourly, 'how you ever made chief inspector.'

'Hard work.'

'And a surfeit of imagination! I tell you, you're talking a lot of rubbish. I've already explained that I was nowhere near the Old Mill that night, I was alone in my digs. I've told you that I long ago sublimated my hatred for Lendon in work. I had no idea he disliked my associating with Cathy. And I never wrote that damned letter.'

'Then who did? And what connection does it have with Lendon's death?'

'That's your problem, not mine. But if you're such a damned clever policeman you'll find out.'

'Cup of coffee?'

Enson's brow contracted at the innocent question. He seemed unwilling to assent, as though by doing so he would be accepting a hand of friendship, but his needs overrode his pride and he nodded reluctantly. Crow rose to his feet and walked out of the room.

He needed to get out for a few minutes. He was puzzled.

Things didn't fit. It had seemed so obvious, so neat as a solution, and yet Enson's stubborn insistence was causing serious doubts to rise. Crow was not given to assessing character by a man's face — he had seen too many prepossessing villains for that — nor by his protestations, and yet there was something about Enson that bore the stamp of truth. Stamp of truth, ring of honesty, name the cliché, and it fitted. But the letter didn't fit.

That letter. Cathy.

Crow asked a constable in the corridor to fetch three coffees from the canteen and then he turned and walked towards the main doors of the station. He nodded to the desk sergeant then went through the doorway to stand on the steps, looking out to the street. It was quiet; there were a few cars about, and a heavy frost had whitened the parked vehicles outside the pub across the way. He stood there, and the night air was sharp to his lungs.

'Cold enough, eh, Crow?'

It was Hugh Simpson. The big, heavy man stood at his shoulder, staring like Crow out into the street. He seemed at ease, and yet there was something . . . after a moment Crow realized that Simpson had been regretting his earlier restrictive attitude towards the inspector and wanted to make amends, but found it difficult to do so.

'How are things going?'

Crow shrugged his narrow shoulders.

'They're not. Bit sticky, really. Puzzling. And you?'

Simpson was silent for a moment. Then as though making up his mind he took a deep breath and said: 'That man Barnes you mentioned. I told you we'd checked him, didn't I? That he was clean? Well, I still wasn't really satisfied, you know, so I went and spoke with his "alibi" — the old porter at the nursing home. Hell, the old man's a dodderer! He'd swear to anything, I'm sure, if the idea was put into his head! And as for dates . . . Still, could mean nothing, except that friend Barnes wasn't around to be interviewed today.'

'You've not found him?'

'He skipped the rest home about lunchtime today, saying he was taking a few days off. His sister hasn't seen him, apparently.'

'He may not be the one.'

'I'm by no means sure he is. There's no record of sexual offences and it's only my suspicion that the old porter—'

'You playing hunches too, Superintendent?'

Simpson scowled.

'We'll see, we'll see. You hanging on with Enson?'

'I've not finished with him yet.'

'Well, maybe I'll see you later. Good night, Inspector.'

Crow wondered what it had cost the burly superintendent to swallow his pride. It couldn't have been easy for the man. Crow shivered. It was cold. He went back into the room to join Wilson and Enson; the coffee had arrived. Crow took his cup and stared at the dark brown liquid despondently.

'Why did you type that letter?'

'I tell you—'

'I said why did you *type* it, instead of writing it in longhand?'

Enson began to continue his denial but caught the gleam in Crow's eye and stopped. In an edgy tone he said, 'I never type personal letters. I have no typewriter at home. The only letters that I get typed are office letters, typed over my signature.'

'That's what I was wondering about. Why should you have typed this one? Could it have been because your hand was shaky? Or was it simply because you couldn't produce Mike Enson's handwriting?'

Enson was staring at him. 'Inspector—'

'No. Let me think out loud for a moment. You couldn't reproduce your own writing, so you type it. But you write your own signature. What does Miss Tennant call you?'

'Mike.'

'Yet you signed your name, *Michael.* Do you always write it in full like that?'

'Yes.'

'Even to Miss Tennant?'

'I've never written to Miss Tennant.'

'Mmm. So you say. Strange, that letter . . . I mean, why did you ask her to *meet* you at the Mill? You both live alone, you have a car, you could have picked her up. Instead you send a typed letter . . . and you sign your full name . . .'

Crow sipped at his coffee, his eyes brooding on Enson's attentive face. It was a nice face really, wide mouth, pleasant slate-grey eyes, but those eyes could be hard and angry, Crow knew.

'Tell me about Cathy Tennant. Tell me where you met her, how you met her, the circumstances. Tell me all about her and your relationship with her.'

Enson looked doubtful; there was a hint of suspicion in his face as though he were aware of Crow's more relaxed, diffident approach.

'I met her in January. We became friendly, were attracted to each other . . . I asked her to marry me.'

'And you quarrelled.'

'That was nothing.'

'But you didn't make it up.'

'Well, she started acting strangely, refused to see me after Lendon died. I couldn't understand why.'

'We know why now. The letter.'

'But I didn't write it! When we quarrelled at the pub I thought she was upset because she'd discovered about my father from Lendon's papers. That angered me. I didn't see why she should cool towards me because Dad went to prison. But I was angry too, especially at the thought of the way your probing would drag it all out again.'

'She ran off from you that night.'

'That's right. Through the woods.'

'You frightened her, chasing her like that.'

'I didn't chase her!' Enson's tone was harsh. 'When she left me at the pub I was so angry I said to hell with it all and I went back to the car and I drove home. Let her walk home, I thought to myself! But chase her . . .'

His voice died away. He sat upright. Suddenly he was staring at Crow like a rabbit hypnotized by the glare of headlights.

Crow knew that the young man's thoughts were beginning to drift along the lines that Crow had already moved along; Mike Enson was just beginning to visualise the picture that Crow was already seeing dimly, hazily and yet with a certain conviction.

'That same evening, earlier,' Crow said with a massive calm, 'you were waiting for Miss Tennant outside her office. You followed her home. We followed you.'

'There was a policeman? Following me?' Crow smiled hesitantly.

'I thought it was necessary to keep an eye on her. I guessed that something was worrying her, and I wanted to know what it was. It was you.'

Enson made no reply. His mouth was set in a grim line, his eyes fixed on Crow. The inspector leaned forward, speaking softly.

'That same evening you called on her and you took her out. You went to the public house above Kenton Wood and you quarrelled again, so she left you and went down through Kenton Wood . . . and she was frightened by someone. I also had occasion to be in the vicinity of the wood that night, I picked her up, as I told you.'

Crow paused.

'After I drove her home that night, a car nosed into the road behind me, You?'

Enson shook his head. He thought for a moment. 'But there was a car parked outside the pub when I left her. Someone was sitting in it: he'd have seen Cathy run into the wood.'

'He?'

Enson shrugged.

'I don't know, I paid little attention. He, she, seemed unimportant.'

'But you're sure there *was* a car there? And its occupant could have seen Cathy go down into the woods?'

'And me going back to my car and driving off. Hell, if only I'd realized that she might . . .'

'That letter.' Crow rose to his feet to tower gauntly above the man in the chair. Wilson rose with him.

Crow grimaced. 'The letter. You say you did not write it. If you did not, someone did, someone who knew your signature—'

'It could be anyone who had received a letter from my office over my signature! Anyone with whom the firm had had dealings!'

'Whoever wrote that letter obviously didn't intend it for Lendon. That man, or woman, wrote it *to entice Cathy Tennant to the Old Mill.* But Lendon got it, and Lendon went, and Lendon died. What would have happened if Cathy had gone? Would *she* have died?'

Enson rose in anxious haste. His glance darted from one policeman to the other as though seeking reassurance, 'But who would want to . . . why would—'

'Cathy didn't go to the Mill, and Lendon died. Then Cathy goes into Kenton Woods and—' The silence grew unbearably heavy, 'It could, of course, have been the same person,' Crow said quietly, 'at the Mill and in the woods. Each time hoping to reach Cathy.'

'Miss Tennant has gone to see Mrs Bell this evening.' Sergeant Wilson spoke for almost the first time that evening.

For a moment Crow hesitated, then he picked up the telephone,

'Squad car, immediately!' Then, replacing the receiver, he added to the two men facing him, 'I wonder whether Mrs Bell did in fact know that Cathy was Charles Lendon's beneficiary? Or if she did not, whether she does now?'

Chapter 21

The car swept through the town with its blue light flashing and klaxon sounding. Crow sat huddled in the back seat beside Enson, who quivered with an impatient nervous energy. Perhaps it had been unwise to allow the young man along, but when he'd agreed to it Crow had glanced at Wilson and seen the message in the sergeant's eyes. He'd handle Enson if there were any angry outbursts. Crow was satisfied; Wilson was reliable.

His palms were sweating in spite of the coldness of the night air. Nervous reaction. Cathy Tennant. How could he have seen that her life was in danger? Was there any time previously when he should have suspected it?

The car hurtled around the corner on screaming tyres.

They swung into Woodrow Lane and the flashing light lit the trees eerily in a bluish white glow; the frost threw back a myriad twinkling blue lights.

Dark marks scarred the frost on the track. A car had come down ahead of them.

When the police car stopped Enson got out quickly and ran for the house, shouting Cathy's name. Crow dragged at the car door; Wilson was already hurrying after Enson.

As Crow came up to the front door Wilson was restraining Enson as the man pressed angrily at the bell push. The klaxon died whiningly and the impassive house remained silent and disapproving.

'Cathy!'

Enson's call was unanswered. Crow gnawed at his lower lip. The house seemed to be empty.

'We'll try the back of the house. Constable . . .?'

'Here, sir,' came the reply at Crow's irritable tone and the driver materialized at Crow's elbow.

'Around to the side, to the garage. See if the car that made those marks is there. And check, if it isn't, to see whether it's been driven into the wood. If it has, you can—'

Crow never finished, and Wilson, heading for the back of the house, stopped dead in his tracks.

'Cathy!' Enson's voice was agonized, for there was no mistaking the scream: wild and tearing, it was the scream of a woman in terror.

Enson was already racing across the frosted garden towards the trees bordering Kenton Wood. Crow shouted and went after him, but even as he did so he caught a flicker of light from the house. He hesitated, then ignoring it, stretched his long legs in pursuit of Enson and Wilson who were already plunging through the trees ahead of him. Above the crashing of their progress came the screaming, again, but this time the panic was shut off, suddenly, brutally.

Hands upon a woman's throat could do that.

Tree branches rimed with frost scrabbled at Crow's shoulders as he forced his way onwards in the direction of the screams. It was intensely dark among the trees in spite of the star-reflecting frost, but just ahead of him was the noise of Wilson's progress. And Enson's. Crow knew now that it had been a mistake to bring that young man. If

203

anything had happened to Cathy and if they caught the person responsible, Crow knew that Enson would tear the assailant to pieces, given the opportunity.

The sounds of crashing progress were changed suddenly; there was only the sound of Wilson's body momentarily, and a cry of absolute rage from Enson. Almost at the same time a light flickered strongly ahead: Wilson. The only one with sense to carry a regulation issue torch from the car. Crow thrust his way forward in time to see the torchlight whirling in wild parabola as Wilson struggled with a thrusting, angry figure. It was Enson. Crow forced his way forward to see a dark, inert mass on the ground and a shapeless form crouched above it. Over them struggled Wilson and Enson.

'Enson!' shouted Crow in a furious tone. The two men stopped struggling as though whipped by a lash and Crow came up to them, to look down at the forms at their feet. There was a curious moaning whimper drifting up to the trees, a dying sound, but Crow could not make out its source. He took the flashlight from Wilson and directed it downwards.

The dark grass and frosty leaves were trampled and black. The inert form on the ground was still, the face white except for the darkness of blood at her throat. Crow felt a freezing coldness in his stomach and flicked the beam towards the man kneeling at Cathy's side.

It picked out with a harsh precision the gasping, fear-torn features of James Carson.

Chapter 22

All she could remember was the stabbing light on her face and the slithering sound; then there was the running, just like that other night in Kenton Wood . . . But now her throat was sore and her head ached and a finger of sunshine was picking its way across the pale coverlet and two men faced her. One was tall, stooping, with a predatory nose and bald skull. His deep-set eyes were friendly. Chief Inspector Crow. And beside him, Michael Enson.

'Don't look so worried, Cathy. He's not in custody.'

'What happened?'

'Explanations can wait until later, You need to rest now.'

'I'll be here when you wake again,' Mike said quietly and smiled at her. The expression on his face caused a warm glow to arise in her. Then he squeezed her hand, and she was drifting again into a warm sunlit sleep.

Quietly, Crow walked out of the room. There were a few more questions he'd want to ask the girl yet, but they could wait. He'd more or less got it all now. He looked up to see Wilson approaching.

'Mr Tennant has arrived, sir.'

'He'll be wanting to see Cathy. She's asleep now, and Enson's with her. I'll have a word with Tennant.'

In the waiting-room Arthur Tennant rose to greet him. There were still lines of anxiety around his pouched eyes. 'Has she come round?'

'Yes, but she's asleep again now, and young Enson's with her. If you have a word with the doctor I'm sure he'll allow you in there. But she'll be all right . . . shock is the problem, mainly.'

Tennant sat down and shook his head in quiet relief.

His yellow-stained fingers trembled slightly as he took out his pipe. Crow felt a surge of compassion for the man.

'When I saw you last night,' Tennant said, 'you weren't inclined to tell me much about what happened.'

'I can tell you now.'

'John Barnes was badly injured?'

'A broken nose and jaw; his cheekbone may be fractured too. But he'll stand trial for the murder of Jenny Carson and the attempted murder of Cathy.'

'And Charles Lendon?' 'And Charles Lendon.'

'But I don't understand how it all happened.'

Crow sat down beside Tennant and leaned back in the chair.

'It all began for John Barnes some years ago. He was brought up in the society of women and I suppose the 'head-shrinkers' will have something to say about that, and sexual repression and so on, but the fact is he had an unhappy love affair which scared him off women sexually. Until he caught Jenny in the woods, there was nothing to suggest that he was abnormal, however.'

'He assaulted her, and killed her.'

'I don't know how often he wandered those woods; I don't know whether he intended what happened. It may have been sudden impulse, but that night Lendon was away in Silchester, Barnes stayed with Mrs Bell, and in the morning walked in the woods — and found Jenny. There's an old porter at Linwood who'll swear that Barnes was there that night, but he's so doddery he'd swear to anything Barnes fed him. And Mrs Bell . . . she's always been overprotective as far as her brother is concerned.'

'You mean she knew he'd killed Jenny.'

'Suspected, at least, but probably knew, yes. She covered for him, certainly.'

'But why did Barnes go after Lendon — and Cathy?'

'For Barnes, I suspect, the floodgates were down once he had attacked Jenny. He wanted a woman, and Cathy became his target. His sister spoke to him of Lendon's interest in Cathy, he was curious, watched for her, and she became the focus for his attention. He wanted her. But it couldn't be like Jenny. He'd have to entice her to a lonely place, perhaps a lovers' tryst. He knew she was seeing Enson. The Old Mill seemed ideal.'

'Did Mrs Bell know what was on his mind?'

'I think she might have guessed later. I suspect he might have come to her after killing Jenny and she told him to go to the nursing home and arrange an alibi with the porter. Easily done; a mention of the time later and the old man at once agreed.'

'How did Barnes think he could get Cathy to the mill?'

'We've been through his room. He's got a dozen sheets of stationery from Enson's firm — and Enson's stencilled signature on some publicity material. He must have visited the firm and lifted some. Anyway, he sent a note to Cathy by leaving it at reception when no one was there . . . from across the street he'd be able to see when the reception office was empty. It was an assignation and purported to come from Enson, though it was signed *Michael*, since it was copied from the stencilled signature, instead of just *Mike*. But his luck was out.'

'How do you mean?'

'Lendon had been out that afternoon with . . . a certain lady. He came in, saw the letter and ripped open the envelope. Barnes couldn't know that Lendon would be interested in Cathy's association with Enson, couldn't know he'd see the letter and intercept it, suspecting it might be from Enson. And he couldn't know that Lendon would then turn up in her place at the Old Mill, to warn Enson away from Cathy. Barnes was already keyed up, bordering on nervous panic at the thought of Cathy coming to him. He was geared to a violent sexual act; the appearance of Lendon must have terrified him, and he's not a strong specimen. Barnes must have panicked. He would have fled, I'm sure, but there was no egress so he hid. Lendon came in, perhaps called, then came forward. Under Barnes's hand was a rusty skewer and as Lendon came in through the inner doorway Barnes stepped forward and with one nervous, terrified blow drove it into Lendon's heart.'

Tennant slowly expelled his breath and sat staring at the pipe in his hand. 'But he still . . . wanted Cathy.'

'Lendon's death solved nothing for him. He still felt a strong, unnatural desire for Cathy, and he burned to assuage it. He watched her, followed her . . . in a perverted sense I suppose he loved her. In the meanwhile Cathy was in a daze. Lendon had stuffed the letter in a file and she'd found it.'

'And assumed Enson had sent it?'

'That's right. In spite of her doubts and fears she went out once more with Enson, however, to the Bear Inn. Barnes followed them. He saw her quarrel with Enson in the car park, he followed Cathy into the woods, and he tried to attack her then. He was almost caught. His sexual frustration was mounting and at last he threw caution aside. He watched her take the bus to Lendon's house, followed in his car. When she spoke to Mrs Bell he entered the house with the key Alex Bell had given him. He hid on the stairs and listened.'

Crow hesitated; he was somewhat reluctant to go on.

'I think Mrs Bell must have heard her brother on the stairs. I suspect that, hearing him, she then sent Cathy out through the back door, and while she sat alone in the house with the lights turned off she must have heard John Barnes leave through the front door. She . . . she must have known what was to happen; she made no attempt to stop it.'

'I don't understand.'

'She was bitter and disappointed. She felt cheated; she'd expected more from Lendon's will. Cathy would have given her the house, but Alex Bell didn't give her a chance to say it.

She left Cathy to Barnes . . . you'd have thought she'd want to protect her brother from such an action, but her desire for revenge against Lendon and Cathy must have overridden her protective instincts. She stayed quietly in the house, even when we came knocking. Barnes went for Cathy when she left the house, shone a torch in her face and went for her. But he must have slipped on the frosty ground for he didn't catch her until she reached the edge of the woods. He struck her with his torch and began to drag her, unconscious, into the cover of the trees. His intention was to rape her and then kill her quietly. But his progress was slow and noisy and he was frightened and excited. He was not too far in before he stopped, and tore open her coat. She began to come to herself, she struggled, she screamed, and Barnes lost control, his sexual motive was overcome by fear. She was a strong young woman, not a child, and he panicked. He began to strangle her; in a few minutes she would have died.'

'Instead of which,' Tennant said feelingly, 'James Carson nearly killed Barnes.'

Crow nodded. Only that morning Mrs Carson had come to him, anxiously, worried about what trouble her husband might have got into in attacking Barnes like that. Crow felt sorry for her; so much evil had come her way.

'We have Carson to thank for Cathy's life,' he said to Tennant. 'We know now that Carson *was* out the night Lendon died. He'd been out almost every night, in the woods since he lost his daughter. Carson was convinced that the killer of Jenny would strike again and he felt the police were doing nothing so he took the law into his own hands. The strange thing is that Carson was almost *drawn* towards the areas where Barnes prowled: It was as though he was impelled by a sixth sense, as though he could smell Barnes's fear and excitement. For he almost caught Barnes the night he chased Cathy down from the Bear Inn. Carson went in to complain, suggest the woods be watched by the police, next morning, in fact. He was turned away. But if he failed to catch Barnes the first time, he didn't fail the second time. And in fury and hate he almost beat Barnes to death, when he caught him strangling Cathy.'

Tennant was staring at his own tobacco-stained fingers. They were clenched tight.

'I know how he felt,' he said.

'When we got there, it was over. Barnes had been battered pretty badly. Carson was kneeling over Cathy when she came to herself and she screamed again because she thought it was Barnes. We had to restrain Enson from attacking Carson at that point.'

Tennant nodded. Slowly he rose and smiled at Crow, but it was a nervous smile.

'I think I'd better go in and see her now. You . . . you know Enson wants to marry her, don't you?'

'She could do a lot worse for herself.'

After Tennant had gone to join Enson, Crow stood on the steps of the hospital waiting for Wilson to bring the car around. He stared at the sky: it looked as though rain was not far off. He now had the task of meeting Chief Constable Rogers and Hugh Simpson. It was not a situation he relished. Simpson could have prevented this last attack if he had only heeded Carson's warning. He could have taken Barnes if he had been less touchy, unyielding in his attitudes. Simpson had been pig-headed and wrong . . . but had Crow himself been free from blame? He had owed it to Simpson, as a fellow officer, to give him all the information in his possession, discuss with him any suspicions he might have . . . but he had failed to do so. All right, maybe Simpson had made liaison difficult, but it was wrong to lay all the blame at the chief superintendent's door. Crow should have overcome his personal feelings about Simpson, should have overridden his own pride and insisted on Simpson listening to him. As it was, their fatal lack of liaison had almost resulted in a third murder.

The car was waiting. As they drove away Wilson asked: 'Will Lendon's ex-partner Philips be proceeded against, sir?'

'On the company frauds? I think so. Certainly for the burglary of the office . . . they can match threads from his jacket with some caught on the window sill.'

'And Dr Barstow?'

'Oh, I think he's for the medical high jump. My guess is, though, that once Mrs Kent is divorced he'll marry her, and shortly afterwards apply for reinstatement. Successfully too, I should think.'

'The Sunday papers will love it all.'

They will, Crow thought. As they'll love photographing Mrs Bell, splashing that handsome face all over the front pages. Crow would have to interrogate her again and he wasn't looking forward to it. She was no longer the woman he had met at Lendon's house, she wasn't the woman who had so impressed him. And yet she was, basically; he had seen the flaws in her make-up then, but had given them insufficient prominence in his mind. He wondered now whether she'd be able to steer clear of the charge of being an accessory to her brother's crimes. It was possible; she was intelligent, resilient, and she had the selfishness to survive at all costs.

A lovely woman. But hard. She hadn't mourned Charles Lendon. For that matter, who had? Cathy Tennant might, once the pain and the questions faded, for she was a sensitive girl. But generally Lendon would remain unmourned.

Still, lawyers usually did.

THE END

Thank you for reading this book. If you enjoyed it please leave feedback on Amazon, and if there is anything we missed or you have a question about then please get in touch. The author and publishing team appreciate your feedback and time reading this book.

Our email is office@joffebooks.com

www.joffebooks.com

More Inspector John Crow books coming soon!
Join our mailing list to be the first to hear about them
www.joffebooks.com/contact/